NAïveté

A JOURNEY OF SECOND CHANCES

KAZUKO SMITH

Copyright © Kazuko Smith 2024

All rights reserved.

No part of this publication may be altered, reproduced, distributed, or transmitted in any form, by any means, including, but not limited to, scanning, duplicating, uploading, hosting, distributing, or reselling, without the express prior written permission of the publisher, except in the case of reasonable quotations in features such as reviews, interviews, and certain other non-commercial uses currently permitted by copyright law.

Disclaimer:
This is a work of fiction. All characters, locations, and businesses are purely products of the author's imagination and are entirely fictitious. Any resemblance to actual people, living or dead, or to businesses, places, or events is completely coincidental.

ONE

February 28, 2018
Wednesday at 10:14pm

Greetings. I hope you don't mind me sending this.
I am new to Facebook, so please bear with me. I was just wondering if we could be friends here. I hope to hear from you soon.
    Have a wonderful day.

No matter how Kate looked at it, the message was odd.
    For one thing, she didn't know any Edward Jónsson. A message from a complete stranger? To her? It wasn't as though Kate had ever spent much time on social media. She checked her messages from family and friends, posted new photos now and then, and that was it. After the divorce, she'd stopped using Facebook completely. Only in the past few years had she begun to pick it up again. So how had this Edward even found her when they didn't share any friends or acquaintances?
    Yet there it was, right there on her iPhone with the rest of her morning emails and texts. *Greetings.*

Sara would tell her it was a scam. And after eighteen years of friendship, Kate trusted Sara more than anyone. Sara would tell her to delete the message right away, and probably send a dozen articles about online scams while she was at it.

And yet…

I was just wondering if we could be friends here. Hope to hear from you soon.

Kate shook her head. "What am I doing?" She muttered. Maybe she was just tired.

As she finished eating, she pushed the message from her mind. She checked her emails and sent replies to those that needed immediate attention. She did her morning stretches and meditation. She worked, and before lunch, she breezed through her daily French lesson.

Just wondering if we could be friends.

The house was quiet, as it had been ever since her kids had gotten old enough to move out. Through the kitchen window, she could see birds splashing around in the garden birdbath, enjoying the unseasonably warm weather. She would have to go out and prune the flower bushes later; yet another hobby she'd taken up to keep herself busy after work. Along with the French, the yoga, the online articles, and the reading.

It was all very structured. Routine, but boring.

Just wondering…

Her eyes drifted back to her phone.

Had it really been that long since she'd had attention from a man? Was that why she couldn't get the message out of her head? Maybe she was a little lonely, but she wasn't unhappy with her life. Besides, the message was so simple. According to Sara, unsolicited hookup messages were usually explicit, and pushy. If he were interested in her looks, he would have already sent more messages. Maybe even an unwanted picture of his own. But more importantly: Why was she still hung up on this?

At least there was work to focus on. IT translation wasn't exciting, but in Palo Alto, Kate didn't have as many chances to speak Japanese as she wanted. Work gave her that connection back. Japanese was comforting; the formality was formulaic and predictable, unlike English, whose rules were confusing and contradictory. Growing up bilingual had been difficult, but now, she made it work.

For a while, work was an excellent distraction. But when she caught her focus slipping toward the end of the day, she gave up resisting her curiosity.

Alright, Kate, think logically. She shook her head slightly and straightened her posture. *Where does he come from? What does he do for a living? Does he really want to become friends with me?*

It was easy enough to check his profile. It was sparse, the barest information, and only a single picture. It didn't seem locked behind privacy—maybe he really was new to Facebook. A little odd, but not unheard of for older people like them. His son's profile was just like his father's: basic information about him and his school, and a single photo.

Kate, you're being ridiculous. Even kindergarteners know not to talk to strangers. Leave it alone. The voice in her head sounded suspiciously like Sara's. Maybe she really did need to get out more.

Kate went to the kitchen and made some tea, then went out to the terrace, sinking down into a garden chair. The evening was warm, but there was a nice breeze. The blossoms of flowers and trees were yet to be seen, but many little buds had begun to peek out from the earth or from branches. In a month, the garden would be painted red, orange, yellow, and green.

3

When was the last time she'd had someone over? Her daughter had called earlier, promising to come home from San Diego on a university break. But that was still two weeks away, and she'd been gone for months. Sara, Jane, and Mary had all been busy too—with work, and with their own lives. They texted regularly, but she couldn't remember the last time she'd seen them in person.

She was only forty-three. She barely even had wrinkles, thanks to her Asian genetics. She felt like she'd turned twenty-one just yesterday, celebrating adulthood with her closest friends. And while that lifelong bond was still there, they'd undeniably drifted apart over the years. And the last time she'd met someone new... especially a man... well. It wasn't worth remembering.

Her tea no longer tasted sweet and refreshing. "Spend some time with your actual friends, Kate," she muttered, heading back inside. "Delete it and forget it. That's what you need to do."

But despite her resolution, when she fell asleep that night, the message remained on her phone.

The next morning was just the same as any other morning. Kate woke up to her usual ringtone and checked for any messages. To her surprise, she only found one message, and it was from Edward.

Thursday at 11:45pm

Greetings. How are you doing? I hope you don't mind me sending you another message. I hope this doesn't sound weird, but I was looking at your pictures,

4

and I noticed your museum photos. Are
you a fan of Picasso? He is one of my
favorite painters of all time. I'd love to
chat about art, if you're interested.

Was that his attempt at starting a hookup message? It
seemed too polite for that. Perhaps she should've been
bothered to learn he had looked through her photos, but then,
she was the one who left them public. It wasn't that odd.

Or maybe you're talking yourself into replying, Kate.

She read the message again. She did love Picasso. When
she'd been younger, full of adventurous energy, she'd visited
the Picasso Museum in Paris a few times. She'd even gone to
the one in Antibes where he'd spent his last years. That trip had
been the reason she'd started learning French, even though she
hadn't been back to Europe in years.

It wasn't just Picasso, either. Van Gough, Renoir, and
Monet–she loved them all. She'd once dreamed of visiting an
art museum in every country in the world, but that dream had
been replaced with realism long ago.

Who were Edward's favorites? It was dangerous to think
about him, but she couldn't help it. It was common sense to be
cautious online—her friends, her kids, anyone would tell her
to delete the messages and move on. She'd thought the same
thing just last night. But they seemed so harmless, and she
couldn't deny that she was intrigued.

*Fine, answer him. But it's on you if he starts asking for photos
or money,* said the Sara voice in Kate's head.

Well, if he was genuine, then he could be patient. She
made him wait as she went through her morning routine, her
work, and—just to prove to herself that she wasn't starved for

5

new conversation—her lunch. Finally, just before she dove back into work, she sent a simple reply.

> Hello, thank you for your
> message. I'm just fine. How are you
> doing?

****

Edward glanced around his office as he opened his laptop. The small room was occupied with many men working at their computers. Some of them were furiously typing, while others stared boredly at the screen, as if they were trying to mentally generate the messages they were waiting for.

Edward looked at the clock on the wall. It was three in the morning–not quite break time, but he couldn't stand to be at the computer any longer. Grabbing his cigarettes and his lighter, he headed outside. He didn't say a word to his coworkers, and they didn't so much as glance up as he brushed past.

He lit a cigarette and drew the first whiff of smoke deep, expelling it in a long lingering exhalation. Early morning dews glistened on the flowers and trees. The air was already warm and humid; not unexpected, even for the dry season, but even after twenty years, Edward couldn't get used to it.

He'd only been nineteen when he came to Kuala Lumpur. He hadn't planned on leaving Iceland behind for good, but here he was, two weeks past forty. So much for his dreams of heading home and starting college.

He sighed, exhaling a mouthful of smoke. Henrik was ready to leave, that was for sure. He'd been ready for two years, in fact–probably longer. His son had a tendency to stew on things in private before he ever brought them up. Edward wouldn't budge, though. They often fought about it. Edward couldn't keep him safe forever, he knew, but damned if he wouldn't try for as long as he could, no matter what Henrik thought about it.

He drew a second whiff of smoke, then a third. The fourth and the fifth in quick succession. His smoking always got worse when he was frustrated. A cool breeze sent a chill through him, and Edward took that as his cue to head back inside. He muffled a cough in his sleeve as he crushed the cigarette, dragging his feet back towards the doors. It was too bad, he thought, that he couldn't trade places with the cigarette.

No one looked up as he headed back to his computer. The distance wasn't surprising. Edward was the only white man among them, after all. They all spoke English, but Edward had never made any attempts to chat with them, and they were happy enough to leave him alone. Aidan's quotas were strict, after all, and they were hardly running a legitimate business.

It was a scam operation, plain and simple. They picked women from Aidan's lists–always a few at a time–and, after gaining their trust and affection, convinced them to part with hefty sums of money before vanishing from their lives. So basic, but it had always been surprisingly effective. Edward always wondered how Aidan found the women on his lists, but he'd never asked. No questions, no problems. That was his philosophy.

Normally, Edward started from the top and worked his way down the list. This time, though, something had caught his eye: a woman in Palo Alto, California, America. If he remembered correctly, Stanford University was located in Palo Alto; Henrik had applied there the other day. If he got accepted, it would make Edward's "getaway" far more feasible. And if he had a contact in Palo Alto, all the better. It was a flimsy excuse for an alibi, but with half the city under Aidan's control, he needed every scrap of hope he could get.

First, though, he needed the woman to respond.

Luck was with him. When he settled back at his desk, the woman—a Kate—had replied to his second message. It wasn't much, but it was a start. More importantly, she'd only replied a few minutes ago. If he was quick, he could catch her in a conversation.

Hello, I'm so glad you replied.
Sorry, I know my messages came out of
nowhere. But my son said I should use
Facebook to make new friends, so I
thought, why not find out what life is like
across the Atlantic?
I'm originally from Iceland, but I
have been living and working in London
for the last 20 years. How about you?
Your profile says you live in California.
What's that like?

A new message came in a few minutes.

It's very nice. I've lived here
for about 20 years, and the weather is
always beautiful.

For a while, they exchanged basic pleasantries. Kate worked in translation, he learned; Edward, as far as Kate was concerned, was the boss of a small investment company. It was a boring alias, but boring meant few questions, and the less he had to say about his made-up backstory, the better. He'd gotten caught in his lies before, back when he'd first started, and Aidan's punishments had been swift and harsh.

> You mentioned Picasso in your message yesterday. Do you like his paintings?

Yea, I love them. I have one of them in my office.

> Really, which one? I've got a couple in my house. One of them is 'Mother and Son' and the other 'Blue Nude.'

You're kidding, that's what I have, 'Blue Nude!'

> You don't say! I can't believe it!

By the time Kate signed off, he had almost managed to stamp out the usual guilt.

How many women had he talked online for the last twenty years? Too many to count. They were usually nice enough: lonely, awkward, and sometimes naive. The most recent one had been a special case, so vulgar that even Edward, who'd long grown desensitized, had felt uncomfortable. Kate was a breath of fresh air in that regard. The sort of woman he would have enjoyed talking to under better circumstances.

"How's the new list working out?"

Aidan, of course, right on cue. It was like the man could hear it every time Edward daydreamed about getting away from him. Fortunately, Edward's shift was over. He grunted, closing his laptop and getting to his feet.

"I found a good one," he said simply, and headed out the door.

****

Kate was in trouble.

Alright, maybe that was dramatic. But she couldn't believe that after such a short conversation, she had signed off with "talk to you later." It hadn't even occurred to her not to until after she'd already gotten a reply.

Talking to Edward had been easy. Comfortable. She didn't have to pretend to be someone else. Her ex, Robert, was a nice and understanding man. But they couldn't have been more different. He'd had no interest in art and culture.

When was the last time she had felt so comfortable with a man? She certainly couldn't remember. For once, she wasn't eager to get back to work. She wanted to linger, to bask in that nice, warm feeling of connection. But reality called; with one last glance at the open message box, she closed the tab, reluctantly pulling up her work.

Right after college, Kate had gotten a low-paying job writing web articles. Writing came easily to her, and she'd enjoyed the quick results of her work, but she'd grown bored of it. Translation did not give her that kind of instant gratification, but Kate loved what she did. Tackling a big project was like climbing a mountain. It required concentration and patience. Finishing felt like reaching the summit. Only after she stood atop all the completed pages did she feel like she could breathe pure air. No other feeling came close.

It was easier to forget about the conversation with Edward

as she worked. Her productivity carried her through the evening. As she made dinner, she debated calling her kids, but Dominique was probably out with her friends, and William–who was studying at UC Irvine–was probably busy studying. She and William were very close when he was younger, but they'd grown distant from each other lately. They both loved her, she knew, but she doubted they wanted to be bothered.

The ring of the doorbell snapped her out of her thoughts, and she frowned, confused. "Just a minute," she called, turning off the oven and heading for the door. She heard a familiar voice before she even opened the door.

"Hmmm, smells good! What did you make, iron chef Kate?"

Kate couldn't believe it. On her doorstep were the very friends she'd been thinking about yesterday: Sara, Jane, and Mary, all of them clamoring for a hug. "I can't believe it! What are you all doing here?"

"Well, I called Jane earlier, and we realized we haven't gotten together in ages. So, we thought we'd surprise you," Sara explained as the group went inside. At forty-three years old, Sara was Kate's oldest friend. Like Kate, she was divorced with two kids in college. They'd met at their oldest children's preschool, and they'd hit it off immediately. Kate had been new to the area, and Sara had helped Kate out whenever she'd needed it. Their children had literally grown up together.

Kate loved Sara's casual outspokenness. More than once, she'd wished to be more like her friend. Leave it to Sara to show up, friends in tow, right after Kate had been feeling extra lonely. Somehow, she always knew.

Sara, Jane, and Mary sat down at the table, while Kate went back to the kitchen to get some wine. She'd never gotten out of the habit of cooking for four, and while she normally saved the extras for leftovers, today it meant enough food for all her guests. When she came to the table, Jane volunteered to open and pour the wine.

"Cheers!"

Lively conversation flowed easily between them. As they ate and drank, Kate felt herself relaxing. She hadn't realized just how much she'd missed them, and she wondered if they'd been feeling lonely, like her. When everyone was almost finished eating the dinner, Jane held up her empty glass. "We need more wine! Do you have more of this kind, Kate? I really like it."

Jane Wilcox, the oldest in the group at forty-five. She was in the middle of a divorce, and she, too, had two children: both boys. Her oldest, Steve, twenty-three years old, was a software engineer at Apple, and her youngest, Mike, twenty-one years old, was starting his junior year at Stanford in September. Jane was like the older sister Kate never had. She loved to help others in any way possible.

"Yes, I put another bottle on the kitchen counter."

"I'll go get it." Mary jumped from her chair and ran to the kitchen. Out of the four of them, Mary was the quietest, but she was one of the strongest people Kate knew. She, Kate, and Jane had met in a cardio class; Kate and Jane had quit ages ago, but Mary still attended. She'd lost her husband three years prior, but she never lost her determined spirit even through her grief. When she set her mind to something, she gave 120%. It was inspiring.

I wonder if they'd like Edward. The thought startled her; she hadn't thought about the conversation in hours. But once it was back in her mind, Kate couldn't stop herself from getting distracted. As the conversation flowed around her, she found her thoughts constantly drifting back to the short chat they'd shared, and the man on the other side of the ocean.

Suddenly, she heard Jane calling her name.

"Kate, what's cooking these days? Kate? Are you listening?"

"Um, did you say something?"

"Yea, I said, what's cooking these days?"

Kate frowned. "What do you mean?"

"You know what I mean. Are you dating someone?"

Leave it to Jane to bring up dating. If there was one thing Kate didn't love about her friends, it was their repeated attempts to help her find new love. "Oh no, I'm not dating anyone. If I were, you would know about it."

Jane didn't give up. "You're still not ready? Even all these years later?"

Kate looked down at her wine. "Um, I don't know…"

Sara chimed in. "Don't worry. I'll find someone for you, Kate. You know I have great luck with men." With that, everyone nodded and laughed.

Around 10:00 pm, Mary said she had to go. Kate felt relieved, then a bit guilty. She had never felt this way with them before, but the easy comfort she'd experienced earlier was gone. Her friends walked to the front door, still chatting and laughing. They bid Kate goodbye–Sara was the last one out, and she stopped to hug Kate.

"Don't worry about it," she whispered. "I'll keep them off your back."

Kate smiled weakly. "Thanks, Sara."

As soon as they were out the door, Kate looked at her phone. There was no message. She found herself feeling disappointed. *Why didn't he send me anything new?* As she asked herself this question, she was taken aback to realize how much she'd been expecting a new message.

Oh my god. What's happening to me?

TWO

March 2, 2018
Friday at 1:32pm

Greetings from London. I hope you're doing well? I was just thinking about our short conversation yesterday.

You said you were half-Japanese, right? Were you born in America? For myself, I decided to see the world and traveled in Europe during my gap year. Ended up here in London and it has been 20 years since. Time flies, huh?

How many times had he typed those same words in the past twenty years? Edward certainly didn't need to look at the script anymore. He'd memorized all the steps long ago.

In the early days, when Aidan had first cornered him, he'd made mistakes left and right. He typed certain messages too early or too late. He sent them to the wrong people. Keeping up with different time zones was a nightmare, especially since he'd been far more focused on trying to escape his self-made nightmare. Even after he'd resigned himself to working for

Aidan, he struggled. There were so many different names, and the worst thing was remembering which woman lived where. These days, he could keep four conversations going in his sleep if he had to.

Edward sighed, rubbing his face. Everything felt like it had happened just yesterday and a thousand years ago at the same time.

The door flipped open, and Aidan strolled in. Aidan was a few years younger than Edward, but he looked at least a decade older with his sun-dried wrinkled face and large beer gut. Not that anyone would criticize his looks. Aidan came from a very powerful family in Kuala Lumpur. His network was vast. One word from him, and people disappeared without a trace. He ran the scam company, not because he needed the money, but simply because (as far as Edward could tell) he enjoyed the thrill of it.

It was a shame, then, that Edward hadn't known he'd slept with Aidan's wife all those years ago.

Aidan scanned the room quickly. As usual, his gaze landed on Edward. He started over, but abruptly, he changed course and went to his own office instead. After ten minutes or so, Aidan reemerged, and continued over to Edward.

"Hey Edward, looking *pensive*," he barked. Aidan's voice was harsh and raspy, as if he had constantly spent the night yelling over nightclub speakers.

"Pensive?" Edward replied softly.

"Right, fucking *pensive*. Didn't think I knew the word, did you, mister aristocrat! Hahaha!" With that, he quickly exited the room, laughing rambunctiously.

Edward silently watched him go. Aidan was a moody man. His mood rose and fell like a seesaw. When he was in a good mood, he was nice to everybody. When he wasn't, he was loud, rude, and mean. He behaved like that to everyone.

Except Edward. He treated Edward like an arch-rival no matter what. Even twenty years later, he constantly reminded Edward of what he'd done, and he never missed a chance to assert his authority. It didn't matter that Edward had lost almost all hope of escape long ago.

He'd been desperate to get out, in the past—so desperate that he'd even thought about hurting Aidan on many occasions. Over time, he'd stopped trying, but now, that desperation was coming back.

One last time. He would try one last time to get out.

****

As night fell silently in Malaysia, a new day was dawning in California. It wasn't an alarm, but the soft ping of a new message that woke Kate. Sleepily, she checked her phone.

Edward.

As she read the message, her sleepiness was replaced with a sense of comfort. Connection.

In college, Kate had found her soulmate: Ken. They connected on every level. She firmly believed that he was the one, that once-in-a-lifetime kind of true love. He'd felt the same way. They'd planned to get married after graduation.

He'd been even more adventurous than her. Kate loved traveling and experiencing new things, but he'd been an adrenaline chaser. One day, he told Kate that he wanted to climb Everest before settling down. He'd said he wanted to impress her. That by climbing the mountain, he would prove their love could also overcome anything.

He never returned. Kate wasn't sure she'd ever gotten over the grief. She'd liked Robert, the man she eventually married, but they'd never shared that kind of connection.

But chatting with Edward brought back that feeling. She started typing a reply, then stopped abruptly. She didn't want him to think she was anxious to chat with him. Desperation was a bad look.

She put the phone on the side table and changed into comfortable clothes, then went to the kitchen. She fixed herself a bowl of oatmeal and coffee and sat down at the table. She took the time to finish her breakfast, then went to the bathroom. She even took the time to check on her garden. The California blue sky spread out endlessly. The flower buds looked mostly unchanged, but she could see the first hints of color from her window. Kate couldn't help smiling and soon found herself humming an indistinguishable tune.

She grabbed her phone on the way to her office and debated replying to Edward. But she had a feeling that if she started talking to him, she would get distracted, and she couldn't afford to lose hours of work.

She worked through the morning, then the afternoon, with only a break for lunch. When the phone rang, she was surprised to see how late it had gotten.

It was Sara. "Hi Kate."

"Hi. How are you?"

"I'm okay. Just wanted to say thanks for a delicious dinner and a good conversation last night."

"You're welcome. Thanks for being good company, as always."

"Speaking of, you were really distracted after a while. What's going on?"

"What do you mean?" Kate said, uncomfortably guilty. She knew what Sara meant.

"Oh c'mon! You can fool the other two, *mais pas moi*. You've definitely got something going on." Kate knew exactly how Sara looked on the other side of the phone. Urgent. Worried, but eager for gossip. Kate hesitated for a moment, but decided to share just a little.

"Well, it's just a little thing. I don't know what's gonna happen…"

"Okay, tell me more." More urgency. Kate could almost feel Sara's intense stare.

"I received a message from someone a couple of days ago," she said. "We just talked a little bit. That's all."

"Hmm… a little thing, huh? But you were so preoccupied last night."

Kate winced. "Was that obvious?"

"Yep!"

"Don't tell the others, okay? 'Cause I really don't know how it's gonna pan out."

"Okay, okay," Sara laughed. "My lips are sealed. But I want a full report in a week."

"Got it, if I'm even still talking to him then."

After dinner, Kate finally made up her mind and typed her reply.

> Good evening (or good morning over there?). To answer your question…
>
> Right after my college graduation, I traveled around a little bit and ended up in the US. Basically, I wanted to see America and other countries firsthand.
>
> And then, poof, 20 years had gone by… time flies fast…

Ping!

Yeah, you can say that again!

Do you have children? I have a son, just
turned 20. He goes to college here.
    I think he wants to be an engineer
just like his old man, haha.

Oh, that's great!

I have two, a girl and a boy.
My daughter is 21, and my son 18.

Both are in college.

Very nice, indeed!

What are their names, if you don't mind
me asking? My son's name is Henrik.

    Henrik? Kate had never heard that one before. She debated
asking about its origin, but decided not to. She didn't want to
get too invested too quickly.

I like the name Henrik. Mine
are Dominique and William.

Good names. Can I ask you a personal
question?

...Sure...

Are you married?

No. I'm divorced.

Oh, I'm sorry.

Don't be. It happened a long
time ago.

I'm not married, either. My wife passed
away four years ago.

Oh, I'm so sorry to hear that.

Thanks. I'm okay. I still have my son,
who makes me happy.

What about you? What makes you
happy?

Kate leaned back in her chair.

What *did* make her happy? Her children, of course, but was that truly all she had left? She loved traveling, but she hadn't done it for a long time. She loved taking photos, but recently, she'd been too busy to go out and take any. She couldn't even remember the last time she'd gone to the movie theater.

Kate leaned further back in her chair, stumped. Another ping came from her laptop.

Are you still there?

> Yes, I'm still here. I was
> thinking.

She frowned. For lack of anything else to say, she typed, *I like kids. Their smiles always make me happy. What about you?*

Kate waited for a few minutes, but no response came. Just as she was about to send another message, he replied.

I like that very much. When my son was little, he was the cutest boy in the neighborhood, because he was half.

> Half? I'm half, too. Half
> American and half Japanese.

That's why you are so pretty.

> Oh, thanks. What about your
> son?

There was another long pause.

He is half Icelandic and half Greek.

Suddenly, Kate's phone rang, nearly startling her out of her skin.

"Who…?" Oh. Her mother. Normally, Kate loved chatting with her, but today, she huffed. She started talking almost as soon as she picked up the call, beating her mother to the punch.

"Hi Mom! How is your trip so far?"

"Hi Kate–Oh, my trip? Just fine. How are you, dear?"

21

"Oh, I'm okay. We girls had a nice dinner here last night."

"Your usual gang, Sara, Mary, and Jane?"

"Yep, them." Kate looked at the clock anxiously. "Sorry mom, did you need something?"

Unfortunately, her mother didn't take the hint. "No, I just missed your voice. Any good news lately?"

"Good news, not really. Same old, same old."

"That's good. If anything comes up, you can always tell me, okay?"

"Um… okay, Mom."

The conversation dragged on. Kate gave half-hearted replies, but she wasn't really listening to her mother. All she wanted was to go back to chatting with Edward–which was a bit of a startling realization. Had she lost all her caution that quickly?

Impatiently, she jumped from her chair, pacing around the room and trying to concentrate on her mother (to no avail). When they finally hung up, she took a deep breath, forcing herself to slow down.

> Sorry, I was on the phone with my mother. Are you still there?

Yes, I'm still here. How is your mum?

> She's fine. She's been traveling around Europe, just like you did. But I worry, since she's not young anymore, so I asked her to call me at least once a week.

Is she traveling alone?

Oh no, she has her friend with
her. So, that's a relief.

You said you love traveling too, right?
You must've gotten it from her.

Kate smiled.

Yeah.

They talked for a while longer. Edward seemed very interested in hearing about her travels; he asked question after question, and Kate found herself telling stories she hadn't thought about in years. By the time they signed off, it was well past Kate's usual bedtime.

You're not being careful at all. But it was harmless, wasn't it? They were only getting to know each other. She couldn't see how anything she'd told him was risky.

Still, she knew Sara would tell her to be cautious. If she told her mother or her daughter, she was certain that they would tell her the same thing. Kate had to remind herself that she was just having a good time chatting with him. Nothing more, nothing less.

****

Another day ended for Kate, and another morning broke for Edward. He settled down in his chair to start his chat with Kate, feeling exhilarated. He had not felt this way for a long time. Not since his son was born. It was a good feeling.

He liked Kate. There was nothing else to it. Under different circumstances, he could've fallen for her for real.

Hi Kate, how are you doing? Hope your
day was great.

> Hi. I'm fine, and my day was
> good. How was your night?

These messages became their signature greetings.

He'd learned many years ago that when men and women first met online, they typically went through several relationship stages. The first stage, according to the manual Aidan had given him, was the "getting to know you" stage. Edward was supposed to ask as many questions as possible. But he was not supposed to freely give his thoughts or opinions unless the woman asked back. Even then, he was supposed to keep his answers to a minimum. In a normal relationship, after the 'getting to know you' stage was over, they decided whether they should start "seeing" each other. This wasn't true for Edward, as he had to continue whether he liked the person or not. It was his job.

Kate made it easy to break the rules, though. Already, he'd had to put the brakes on his own words, lest he say something he shouldn't.

Edward glanced at the clock on the wall. It was almost time for her to go.

Do you believe in online dating?

Edward waited for her response.

> Um... I don't know if I do or
> not. I mean there are many scammers
> out there these days. So, you need to
> be careful.

Right. But there are lots of people really
looking for love, too.

> Do you think so? I hope so,
> anyway.

I do.

I actually know a few couples who've
met online, and they're all living happily
ever after.
    I believe people can find their
soulmate online if they have faith.

> Come to think of it, I know
> some couples, too.

See?

> Can I ask a question?

Sure.

> Why did you send me a
> message in the first place?

I told you before that I was looking for a
friend.

> I remember that. But why me?

Edward hesitated. He stared at the screen for a long time.

Well, it is because I liked your face. But don't get me wrong. Yes, you are pretty. But that's not really what I meant...

Hmmm... how can I explain?

I see goodness in your face. I thought that if anyone would respond to me kindly online, it would be someone like you.

THREE

O ver the next few days, Kate and Edward settled into a routine. They chatted for hours, each night (for Kate) and each day (for Edward). Conversation flowed naturally between them, and somehow, they didn't run out of things to talk about. After only a week, they talked as if they had known each other for a long time. At the end of the seventh day, Edward had a confession to make.

Kate, I have something to tell you... I think I'm in love with you.

> What, wait a minute?! Aren't you moving too fast? We have only known each other for a week. How can you say that?

I know. I realise we just met. But I know when I found true love. I can't deny this feeling.

Edward couldn't believe himself. This wasn't part of the

script. Of course, he had to confess his "love" eventually, but not after one week of chatting. He'd never done this before. But when he thought of his escape plans, he couldn't help his feelings of urgency.

Hello, are you there, Kate?

> Yes, I'm here. I don't know
> what to say, really. I'm stunned.

Sorry, I didn't mean to confuse you. Just wanted to tell you how I feel...

> Well, you confused me
> alright...

Sorry.

Suddenly, the door flew open, and Aidan burst in.

Kate, I gotta go. I'll talk to you tomorrow.

Everybody quickly returned to their screens so as not to face their boss. Edward, on the other hand, looked up from his screen and toward the door. As expected, Aidan was coming for him.

"Hey Edward!"

Edward steeled himself. He looked up, feeling defiant. "Yeah?"

"How's it going with the new girl, huh? That American you mentioned last week."

"It's going well, I suppose..."

"Let me see." Aidan pushed him aside to look at the screen.

Edward sat very still, keeping his expression neutral.

"What the fuck?! You already told her you're in love? Why the fuck are you confessing so early, man?"

"I know, the manual says to wait."

"I asked *why* the fuck so early?"

"I don't know, I just felt like it…"

"It's your lucky day, 'cause I'm in a good mood. But stick to the manuals, you got that?"

"Yes, sir."

"Hmph. keep up the good work, man!" Then, Aidan walked to the next row and started yelling at someone. Eventually, he left the room.

Such conversations had happened many times over the years. No one but Edward dared to contradict Aidan. He argued with Aidan on many occasions, even though he knew it only made his situation worse. As long as his men conducted their work according to the manuals, Aidan didn't care what they did. He barely even came to check on them, but he always knew when someone was expecting money. He never missed those days.

Edward always thought there was no way for Aidan to know who was getting money when he wasn't even in the office. How could he know? He was their direct supervisor, and Edward had never seen anyone who looked like a manager or an assistant take over while Aidan was away. Yet every time, Aidan came back knowing exactly who had done what. Eventually, Edward figured out that Aidan must've had an informant in the office who discreetly reported to Aidan on a regular basis.

This thought disgusted Edward so much. He hated the feeling of being watched without knowing it. He had to get out of there.

****

I think I'm in love with you.

After Kate's divorce, her friends had tried to help her start over. They'd fixed her up on a handful of dates. She'd humored her friends, but she never felt comfortable with any of the men she went out with. She only saw most of them a few times. One had said that he was in love with her after a month or so. Her response? She just told him that she was not ready for a serious relationship. They'd broken up shortly after.

Kate just couldn't be spontaneous with her relationships anymore. She needed a lot of time to think before she made a decision. That was true even with men she'd met in person, let alone online. There was just no possible way for her to accept a love confession from someone she had only "met" a week ago.

Maybe he's teasing me. But as soon as she thought about it, she realized something much worse.

Edward was a scammer. How else could he say that he was falling for her?

Just to be sure, she typed "romance scam" into the search bar. The results came up instantly.

"Romance scammers will express strong emotions for you in a relatively short period of time... they often come from western countries but are working overseas," Kate read a few lines. Her heart sank. "He fits right in."

Restless, Kate went outside to her garden. She walked around, trying to get her thoughts in order.

One day she received a message from a man. Naturally, she dismissed it at first, but to her surprise, she found herself still talking to him after an entire week. She wondered what sort of trick God planted to keep the conversation going, but one thing was clear: She could be completely herself when she conversed with him. They talked about everything, from art to travel, to happiness and fear. Edward was a good listener, but he was still enough of a stranger that Kate found it easy to tell him many things she couldn't tell other people, including her friends.

But when she was not talking with Edward, her doubt toward him returned. He could be a scammer. She was a smart woman–she knew better than to trust this. And yet, she couldn't help gravitating toward him.

"No, no, no... we only met a few days ago," Kate reminded herself. "This feeling is not love. That's for sure."

...Or was it?

Her thoughts went back and forth between acceptance and denial. Finally, she gave up. She couldn't work this through by herself, and Sara had asked for a full report anyway.

Kate went back inside and grabbed her phone. She saw Sara's phone number on the home screen–a recent missed call. She tapped the number.

"Hi Sara, I'm returning your call. It's funny. I was just thinking about calling you, but you beat me." The words came out in a rush.

"Of course I beat you. I want a full report, remember?" Kate could hear Sara's laugh. "So, what's been happening?"

Kate took a breath, her heart pounding. "Well, we met on Facebook. We've been talking every night for a few hours. Can you believe that? Time goes fast when we chat. And more importantly, I feel comfortable."

"A few hours every night!" Sara sounded impressed. "What do you guys talk about?"

"A lot of things. He... asks a lot of questions. Ones that make you think about life."

"Like, reevaluating your life?"

"Yes, exactly."

Sara saw right through her. "And now you are falling for him?" She didn't wait for an answer. "You said you met on Facebook? How?"

Kate knew what Sara would say. She could picture Sara's exact expression. Still, she admitted, "He sent me a message, asking to be friends."

"Where is the careful and methodical Kate?"

"I know. But I'm having such a good time chatting with him. Well, I was… at least until last night…"

That got Sara's attention. "What happened last night?"

"Well… he said he was in love with me…"

"In *love*?"

"Yeah. Can you believe that?"

"Hmmm… seems kind of fishy." It was exactly what Kate had expected her to say, but it hurt to hear anyway. "It might be a scam. You'd better slow down, Kate."

"I know, I know. I even looked up romance scams online, and he seems to fit the bill."

"See? Kate, I really want you to think logically here. He said he wanted to be friends, which we all know is never true. And what do you know, a week later, he's confessing his love? You gotta be kidding."

Sara was right. Who confesses their love to someone they met online? After only a week?

"Yeah, you're absolutely right. But… it's been so long since I felt this kind of connection."

Sara was quiet for a minute. "Hey, let's have dinner this weekend with the girls. We can go to our Italian place. Sounds good?"

"Okay. Thanks, Sara."

After they hung up, Kate went back to the terrace. As she gazed at her garden, she weighed two things in her mind: the joy of talking to Edward, and the potential danger–and pain–of being scammed. She had no proof that Edward was a scammer, but no proof that he wasn't.

She had to meet him in person. That was the only way to know the truth.

Ping!

Wednesday at 6:45pm

Hi Kate, how was your day? Hope it was great. Are you there?

Edward was on time for their daily chat. Kate debated replying, but before she could, another message came.

I hope you're not angry about my confession. I surprised myself too. But I wanted you to know.
  Are you there?

Kate hesitated for a few minutes, then made up her mind.

Hello, I'm here. No, I'm not angry, just shocked and confused...

I'm glad. The last thing I want to do is upset you. Sorry to have made you confused, but I meant what I said last night.

But how can you be certain after only a week?

When you find true love, you know it. Time doesn't matter. Do you believe in love at first sight?

I'm not sure if I do anymore. I
used to believe it when I was young.

Well, I believe in it. Remember when I
asked you to send me a better picture of
yourself?
   When I saw the one you sent, I
instantly fell in love with you.
   I think I knew even before that. I can
tell from the way you write that you are
a caring person with a good heart. Good
looks and a good personality? That's a
rare find. But you have both, and that's
why I fell for you.

Kate read his long message repeatedly, trying to detect
anything that could be a scam. She couldn't find anything.
Surely if he wanted something from her, he would have asked
by now, right?
   Kate looked around her office. The mahogany desk that
she has been using for more than ten years, the desk lamp that
was a gift from her ex, the beige leather sofa, and even the tall
plant in the corner–typically, it was all so familiar. Comforting.
But not tonight. Tonight, she felt like she was in a place that
she had never been before. Shakily, she sat down. Several more
minutes passed by, until she heard a ping.
Why aren't you saying anything?

I'm thinking. I've been
thinking all day.

You know, things are moving

way too quickly, and I'm not comfortable with the direction we're heading. Comfort and honesty are two of the most important things to me.

I want to be honest here, Edward. I looked up romance scams online, and you seem to fit in.

My best friend thinks so too.

Me, a romance scammer?! That's a good one!

You really think a scammer would spend hours talking to someone without asking for more personal information? And they would most certainly not confess their love so quickly.

Trust me, I know how suspicious it sounds–I wouldn't have told you if I wasn't dead serious.

Kate, you can read all you want online and talk to as many people as you want, but in the end, you have to decide for yourself. I want you to listen to your heart, because it doesn't lie.

I wouldn't be here if my intentions weren't serious.

Your intentions?

Yeah.

I think I've achieved quite a lot in my life

so far, and I don't need anything from anybody.

But I'd like to find a woman who will love me. Who I can love for the rest of my life...

Anyway, I am sorry if I made you feel uncomfortable. I only wanted to tell you how I felt. Forgive me if I'm moving too fast...

Kate sat for a while, pondering. Finally, she made up her mind and typed.

I understand your intentions.
And I... understand your need for love, too.

Honestly, I have been feeling the same way for a while.
I have family, friends, a good job, everything I need-but not love.

But I really need you to slow down.

I understand. I'll try.

Can we... talk like we normally do?

What did you do today? Did you eat dinner already?

Yeah. Thanks for being so
understanding.

I worked all day as usual and
yes, I already had my dinner.

What did you eat?

They talked a little more, then said good night.

But Kate couldn't sleep, Edward's words echoing in her mind. *Listen to your heart, because it doesn't lie. I don't need anything but love right now. When you find true love, you know it.*

It was all exactly how she felt. If she really did listen to her heart like he said, then she suspected she, too, would be halfway in love with him. But her logical personality told her to be cautious, that she should not make any decisions until they met in person. She'd gone through too much heartache to be hasty.

For the next few weeks, their routine continued as normal. They talked for hours every day. Kate found herself making sure she was online whenever Edward was around so that she wouldn't have to wait for his replies. If it weren't for the way he affected her heart, Kate could almost forget the awkwardness of their past conversation. It hardly felt real.

But the peace didn't last.

Kate, I'm not sure if I can keep my
promise anymore. I think about you all
the time, day and night.

Kate hesitated, but she had to be honest.

...I think of you every day, too.

But honestly, I think we are
just in love with this fantasy we've
created.

None of this is real, you know?

It's not a fantasy. The feelings I have for
you are very real.
You are my soulmate, Kate. I know
it.

A soulmate? How do you know
if someone is your soulmate?

You connect with that person on all
levels. Just like how I feel about you. I
trust my heart.

I trust my heart. How could he say that even after the losses
he'd suffered? How was it that he didn't feel the need to be so
cautious, like she did? Kate's heart and head ached. Her feelings
warred with her logic. She didn't answer, and eventually, the
sound of a new message rang through the room.

You know, I have been seriously thinking
about coming to see you. Wouldn't that
be nice?

There are so many things we could do
together.

We would go for a walk in the park
holding hands.

We would go bike riding or hiking in the
woods and have a picnic. We would go
to a nice restaurant by the sea and look
at the sunset.

Kate was in tears by the time she finished reading. That
was what she missed most: going on a date with someone she
loved. She missed little moments like holding hands, cuddling,
talking. How she wished all the things Edward mentioned
could happen! Her imagination felt like a runaway train, and
she couldn't control her emotions any longer. She cried
uncontrollably for a long time.

Kate, say something...don't go silent on
me...

Taking a deep breath, Kate shook her head as if to shake
off all the romantic feelings that had engulfed her. With
shaking hands, she typed out a response.

...it would be lovely if we could
do all the things you said...

But I still think we are moving
too fast.

I still think we are in love with
this romantic fantasy world we've
created.

Maybe we should cool off.

FOUR

K ate had a good life before she started the chat with Edward. She was in control of her life. She made decisions. She made choices. She was an independent and headstrong woman. She'd suffered too much from love to let emotions drive her any longer. But Edward's confession broke something inside her. She was no longer able to control her emotions. She cried easily and often. It was a real surprise to her to discover her vulnerability this way. Edward continued to send messages day and night, but she just read them and did not say anything back.

Three days after she stopped replying to Edward, her daughter came home. Kate ran to the door as soon as the doorbell rang.

"Hi Mom!" Dominique was all smiles. She'd tanned slightly since Kate had last seen her and trimmed her long, dark hair. She looked like she was enjoying life and was not afraid of anything.

"Hi Dominique!" Kate smiled back, hugging her daughter. As soon as she stepped back, the young man beside her stepped forward and extended his hand to shake Kate's.

"Nice to see you again, Mrs. Fleming." Tren was tall, with

a polite, easygoing smile. He and Dominique had been dating for three years, and Kate had liked him from the very first time they met. He was intelligent and kind, and Dominique was so happy with him.

"It's great to see you too, Tren! It's been too long."

"Come on in, come on in." Kate urged them inside. "Are you two hungry?"

"Yeah, a little bit, huh?" Dominique turned to Tren, who nodded.

"Good, let me fix you some sandwiches. Go sit down. You must be tired from your long drive. I hope you like tuna, Tren," Kate called over her shoulder as she headed for the kitchen.

"Yeah, I love it," Tren replied.

"Mom, don't worry. He eats anything, everything," Dominique chimed in. Kate looked over her shoulder and saw Dominique wink at him. They smiled at each other. Quietly, Kate left them to it.

Shortly after, they settled in to eat. As they talked, Kate realized why Dominique wanted to come home. She couldn't wait until her graduation to show off her new boyfriend.

"Why don't you guys rest upstairs after you finish your lunch? I've got to do a bit more work, okay?"

"Yeah, Mom. We'll do that."

"Thank you for lunch, Mrs. Fleming, it was delicious!" Tren seemed like he meant it.

"Oh, it was nothing. I'll cook something good tonight, okay? Now, go relax," Kate said, already moving toward her home office.

As Kate sat down at her laptop, she thought of Edward. Before, she would've been excited to tell him about her daughter's arrival. But she had not said anything to him in days, even though Edward continued to message her. He often

41

ended with gentle encouragement about trusting herself, having faith, and living life. *Forget about it,* she told herself. *I've got work to do.*

With that, Kate dove into her work. Eventually, the house grew quiet; Dominique and Tren must've fallen asleep. Kate worked through the afternoon and evening until her phone rang. The caller ID said *William.*

"William? Are you okay?"

"Hi Mom, I'm okay. Have you started cooking dinner yet?" William spoke rather quickly.

"I was about to start when you called me. Why?"

"Oh, perfect! I'll be home for dinner tonight. Can you make extra? I'm bringing someone."

Kate frowned, puzzled. "Okay, who?"

"You will see. I've gotta go, so see you in about two hours. Bye!"

Kate started to speak, but William had already hung up. Kate looked at her phone. *First Dominique, now William? We're in for a lively weekend.*

Kate hurried to the kitchen. She had already planned to make salmon, pasta, and salad for Dominique; the kids were lucky she always bought extra.

For the next two hours, Kate busied herself in the kitchen. When all the food was ready, she headed into the garden. The flowers had finally begun to bloom, so she cut a few for decoration. By the time she set the table, brought out the food, and found the perfect spot for the vase, it was already seven thirty. The front door opened; Kate looked toward it and saw William and a girl with long brown hair coming inside.

"Hi Mom! We are here!"

William had always been tall, even as a child. Now, at eighteen, he was a solid 5'10". Kate thought William resembled her more than his father, though William's hair was lighter.

"Hi William! Perfect timing as usual!" Kate looked and sounded excited.

"Mom, I want you to meet Laura."

"Hi Laura, I'm Kate. Nice to meet you."

Laura peered up at Kate through her bangs and offered her a timid smile. Kate noticed light freckles on her face. "Hello, Mrs. Fleming. Nice to meet you, too. Thank you for having me for dinner tonight," Laura said, blushing.

"You're welcome. Come sit down. I'll go get Dominique and her friend." Kate started upstairs.

"Is Dominique here?" William sounded excited.

"Yes. I wanted to tell you on the phone, but you hung up so quickly, as usual. She arrived a few hours ago with her friend, they've been resting upstairs."

Dinner was excellent, and it was a happy one with so many people. The four young people hit it off right away and talked the night away. Looking at them, Kate couldn't help wishing Edward were there too. His presence would have made the happy picture a perfect one. Kate could feel her resolve crumbling; she knew she would send him a message later.

"Thank you for a wonderful dinner, Mrs. Fleming. It was so good!" Laura looked happy and sounded honest.

"Yea, it was excellent, thank you so much!" Tren added, without missing a beat.

"Oh, you're very welcome. I'm glad you both liked it. Hey, I've got something to do, so, will you guys please excuse me?" Kate stood up, smiling.

"Okay, Mom, don't worry about the dishes. We'll clean them up," Dominique promised, already getting up from her chair.

"Yeah, go do your thing. We'll make your kitchen spic and

span in no time!" William was beaming. As Kate went up the stairs, she looked back over her shoulder at Dominique and William. She felt content knowing that both of them grew up to be nice and caring children, despite their parents' divorce. Kate was grateful.

Kate entered her home office and made sure to close the door behind her. When she sat down at her laptop, she pulled up Facebook–and sure enough, there was a message from Edward. He never missed sending his messages. It should've felt pushy, but Kate thought it was very sweet.

I think evening is the perfect time to unwind and reflect on a busy day. I love looking at the sunset and feeling a nice breeze. It helps me settle my mind and focus on one thing at a time. Don't you think so?

I hope you're doing well, Kate. I miss you very much.

Kate didn't realize until just then how much she had missed him, too. She missed his kindness and his wisdom. She even missed his criticism. Edward wasn't just a sweet talker; he challenged what Kate said, and told her honestly that it was hurtful when she left their conversation without saying goodbye. Surely a scammer wouldn't do that, right? A scammer wouldn't risk upsetting her like that. Such thoughts were the reason Kate often felt that she and Edward had a true relationship–but the online nature of it, and Edward's suspiciously quick love confession, held her back.

Hi Edward, I'm okay. Sorry I

haven't said anything for the past few
days, I've been busy.

It's okay, I'm just happy you're back. I
missed you so much, I was going crazy,
haha.

I've missed you too. But I
needed some time to think about
what's really going on between us.

Okay...

Well... I think we should meet
and see what happens.
Online, we can just keep
playing in our fantasy world forever. But
when we meet in person and reality
hits, we may find each other different
from what we thought we were...

Hmmm...

I understand what you are saying, but I
can assure you that my feelings will not
change even when we meet in person. I
know that for sure.

You are the one I've been looking for.
The one I want to spend the rest of my
life with.

I'm serious about this. Can you believe
me?

You want to spend the rest of
your life with me?! No, no, no, you are
jumping ahead again!

I just barely decided I wanted
to meet you, and now you are talking
about a lifetime commitment...

I know. But please understand where
I'm coming from.
It's like I keep saying–I trust my
heart. I know when I've found true love.
It wasn't my intention to find the love of
my life on Facebook, but miracles
happen and you are the miracle, Kate.
I've found one, and that is you.

But we haven't even met in
person yet. You can't be sure.

Things may turn out differently
when we meet in person.

I'm sorry, Edward, but I can't
make up my mind about us until we
meet face to face.

It's okay, you don't have to decide right
now.

But remember I love you, and my feelings will not change no matter what happens.

I know you trust your heart, Kate.

Can you trust me too?

Kate wished she could say yes. But she just couldn't.

"Hey mom, we're finished cleaning." Dominique's voice made her jump—without thinking, she slammed her laptop shut and turned around. Dominique looked surprised.

"Weren't you in the middle of something?"

"Um, it's okay. I just finished what I was doing," Kate said, but she knew she sounded distracted. Dominique didn't look convinced.

"What were you doing? Talking to someone?"

"How did you know?" Kate said, amazed.

"Ah-hah, I was right. Who is it?"

"No one you know." Kate paused. She had a feeling she knew what Dominique would say, but it felt wrong to keep secrets from her daughter. Besides, Dominique was young—she would know more about online dating than Kate did. "Dominique, do you have a minute?"

"Yeah, sure."

Kate spent the next fifteen minutes or so explaining the situation with Edward. Dominique listened attentively without asking any questions. When Kate finished, Dominique did not say anything right away.

But soon she said, "Mom, the whole thing sounds a bit fishy to me. Then again... I know online dating's pretty popular these days. Some people even get married. So, I think as long as he makes you feel comfortable and happy, it's fine." She smiled. "I want you to be happy, you know. Just give it a try and see what happens. But promise me one thing: Whatever you do, do *not* send money, okay?"

Deep down, Kate knew that she would've found an excuse to keep talking to Edward no matter what. But hearing Dominique's reassurances lifted a heavy weight off of her chest. Dominique was so smart--if she said it was okay, then she was probably right.

Kate would be smart, though. As long as Edward agreed to meet her, she could trust him.

"Thanks, Dominique. I really appreciate it. I promise I will never send any money!"

As soon as Dominique left the room, Kate opened her laptop back up. It had gone to sleep in the time they'd been talking, and she tapped her foot impatiently, waiting for it to reload.

Sorry, I was speaking with my daughter. Are you there?

Yeah, I'm still here.

I really wish you'd tell me when you leave. I worry whenever you vanish like that.

Sorry. I'll try to remember.

Kate took a deep breath. She had to be clear and straightforward. It was the only way she could know for sure if Edward was trustworthy.

Edward, I need you to listen

without saying anything for a bit. Okay?

Okay.

Thanks.

You keep asking me to trust
you. To trust my heart.

And maybe it's that easy for
you.

But it's not for me.

I've never had a long-distance
relationship before. And I've certainly
never met anyone online.

I want to believe in you. I
mean, we've talked so much! I think we
know each other pretty well by now. But
I need more than that.

I need more than words. I
need reassurances–to be able to see
you and touch you in person.

You said we could meet,
remember? Everything you described,
that's what I want.

My daughter told me to give
you a chance. And I want to. But

"trusting my heart" like you said... that
means waiting until I see you in person
to decide if these feelings are real.

So... I need you to promise
that we can meet. Otherwise, I'll just
have to let you go.

There. She'd done it. All at once, emotion rushed up inside her, and Kate felt the sudden urge to cry. She stood up and paced around the room to calm down. The longer Edward took to reply, the more nervous she became. When she heard the ping of a message, she dove for her computer.

I understand what you are saying, Kate.

I wish I could come see you right now. I
really do.
But my company is at a very critical time
now, so I can't leave the country. Please
understand.

Kate frowned.

What do you mean "a critical
time?" Is everything okay?

Yeah, everything is okay. It's just that we
have a really big contract that we're
working on, and I have to stay here until
it goes through.
It's really big. It could affect my

whole company. If not for that, I swear I
would come see you right away.

Doubt warred with guilt in Kate's mind. If he was telling
the truth, then she was being so selfish. But if he was making
up an excuse... How could she know what to believe?

> Oh, I see. Sorry about my
> nagging...

It's okay. I completely understand how
you feel.
In the meantime, just think about all
the things I will do for you when we
meet. Think about the happy moments
we'll spend together.

The tears she had been holding back finally began to fall.
It wasn't just Edward–it felt like all of the tears from her past
loves pouring out of her. She hated feeling so confused.

Please, Kate. Can you trust me?

Kate didn't answer. She buried her face in her hands and
cried.

FIVE

"Kate, you want to tell me what is going on?"

The warm afternoon sun cast a long shadow in the living room. Kate's mother, Miki, had just returned from Europe, and they were having tea and cake as they caught up. Miki Smith was seventy years old, a widower, and a no-nonsense woman. She was down-to-earth, just like Sara–Kate used to joke that Sara was her long-lost sister. Miki was also very perceptive–she knew her daughter well. So, after she'd finished giving Kate her souvenirs and telling stories about her trip, she'd turned her attention to Kate.

Kate tried to look nonchalant. "What do you mean?"

"Kate, you've got something going on. I can tell." Miki was clearly determined to find out. Kate had never been able to keep secrets from her mother. She hesitated, but decided to tell the truth.

"Well… I met someone… but online…"

As she explained the situation, Miki listened quietly. It was obvious that she had a thousand questions, but she only nodded now and then, letting Kate talk uninterrupted. When Kate finished her story, she spoke up right away.

"When are you going to see him, huh?"

"Well, I don't know yet. He said he'd tell me tonight."

"Kate, you are a smart woman, and I know you will not do anything foolish. So, I won't say anything… but whatever you do, do not send him money, okay?"

"Yes, I know. Dominique said that, too."

"That's my granddaughter. She is such a smart girl." Miki looked proud; she'd always loved Dominique. "Anyway, it's about time you met someone new. It's been over ten years since the divorce, and you're not getting any younger. If you keep this up, you'll be here all alone as a shriveled old husk!"

"Thanks for the honesty, mom. That's definitely what I needed." Kate shook her head. "Where did you even learn that phrase?"

"Oh, I just learned it from my English friend, so I'm using it. Use it or lose it, you know."

"Right. You're staying for dinner, right?"

"No, I have a couple of friends coming over. But I'll be back for lunch tomorrow."

As Miki left, Kate let her thoughts turn to Edward. A few weeks had passed since Kate had told Edward what she wanted; stuck in limbo, they'd tried to go back to having safe, polite conversations, but it wasn't the same. But at last, Edward had told her he could give her an update.

Kate planned to hold him to it.

****

"Hey, Henrik, I'm home. Are you back?" Edward shouted as he entered the house.

"Yeah, Dad, I'm back," Henrik shouted back, as he came running down the stairs. Henrik had been traveling in Europe for the past two weeks; he'd called Edward on the way home from the airport, so Edward had taken an early lunch and hurried home to see his son.

At twenty years old, Henrik looked very much like Edward with the same height and same build. Henrik's skin and hair were a little darker, but otherwise, it was easy to tell they were father and son.

"How are your grandparents?" Edward asked as they sat down. Henrik had gone to visit them in Iceland and toured some Scandinavian countries on the way back to Malaysia.

"They're good, we went to a bunch of cool places. I wish you could've gone, dad."

"I know. Me too. I haven't seen them in ages." Even if Aidan would've let him leave the country, which Edward doubted, he didn't want Aidan to know anything else about his life or his family. The last thing he needed was yet another way for Aidan to keep tabs on him. But Edward shook off his homesickness and smiled at his son. "Tell me everything about your trip!"

Henrik did. They sat at the kitchen counter and talked for as long as Edward could manage, but eventually, the clock read 10:00 am. He was already running late–Kate would probably be understanding, but he didn't want to give her any more reasons to doubt him.

"Hey–sorry, but I have to get back to the office. Why don't you rest a little? I'll be back in a few hours and we can have your favorites for dinner, how's that?"

"Okay, Dad. Will do."

With a quick hug goodbye, Edward hurried back to the office. Being close to the equator, Malaysia was hot and humid year-round. Edward especially hated the dry season, when the temperatures could hit the lower 90s. By the time Edward reached the office, he was profusely sweating.

He hoped Aidan wasn't around, but when he stepped inside the office, he saw him talking to someone. Edward swore under his breath, then quickly went to his chair and sat down to start up his computer. As he guessed, Aidan quickly came to his desk.

"Hey Edward, how you doing man? How's your new girl?"

"Fine. I was just about to see if she's around."

"I heard she's the only one you're talking to right now. Is that so?" Aidan bent down, peering at Edward's screen. Luckily for Edward, the computer was still booting up, which gave him time to scramble for an excuse.

"Well, she's pretty clingy, so I have to talk to her a lot. I haven't had time to start another one yet." It was weak, but it was the best he could think of on the spot.

"Edward, I think I've been pretty nice to you. I gave you a place in this country that you just *loved* so much. I take care of your kid. Even helped him get into college, remember? All I ask is that you do your job, right?"

Edward felt frozen with fear. It was far from the first time Aidan had lorded his power over him, but every time, it scared him. He had to protect Henrik, after all.

Fortunately, it seemed like Aidan was in a charitable mood, because he just clapped Edward on the shoulder. "You know you've gotta talk to more than one person at a time. We're running a business here. Start another one today. You got that?"

Edward nodded reluctantly. Aidan hung around the office a little longer, so Edward pretended to look through the list as he waited for his boss to leave. When Aidan finally left the room, Edward quickly began typing a message to Kate. Aidan's interruption had cost him; he was an hour late now.

Hello, sorry I'm late today. I hope you
had a good day.

There was no response.

Kate, are you there?

Still no reply. And suddenly, his screen went black.

****

He hadn't shown.

Kate had done her best to trust him. She'd waited as long as she could before she had to face the facts: Edward wasn't coming. Which most likely meant... he had lied. He'd probably never made any plans to see her.

Once the doubts started, they were impossible to stop. *He never actually wanted to talk to you. He probably doesn't even like you. You're just one of a hundred girls he sent that first message to. You were just the idiot who thought it could be real.* When the ping of a message finally came, Kate could barely bring herself to look at it.

"I hope you had a good day?" Is that all he has to say? She couldn't take it; she needed to walk away. She went to the kitchen to refill her wine glass and sat down at the counter. She sat there for a little while, trying to get her emotions under control.

Eventually, she went back to the office. The message was still open on her screen, but Edward had not said anything else. Apparently, that really was all he had to say.

"Well, if he's gonna be that way, then it's his turn to wait for me," she muttered, closing the laptop. She left the office for the second time and went to the living room. What she needed was a distraction, so she stretched out on the couch, turned on the TV, and headed to Netflix.

When her chosen movie was over, it was almost midnight. She turned off the TV and hesitated, wondering if she should check her messages or just go to sleep. Curiosity won out, but when she checked her phone, there were still no messages from Edward.

Well, fine. He could just be that way.

When Kate woke up the next morning, she had a few messages–one from William asking her about the best brand of laundry detergent for girl's clothes, and one from her mother saying that she couldn't come over for lunch, as she would be having friends over. None from Edward.

By now, Kate had progressed from hurt to angry. Clearly, her silent treatment had tipped him off–he must've known she was upset. He hadn't even tried to lie, or placate her. He'd chosen to avoid her. Any sleepy, generous thoughts she'd had about checking in with him vanished.

All day long, Kate was frustrated. She couldn't concentrate on her work. Every time she let her thoughts wander, they went back to Edward. They'd connected so deeply. Why had he suddenly thrown it all away?

The day turned into evening, then night, but still no message from Edward. By the time she finished her dinner, Kate was restless and did not know what to do. Edward had to be ignoring her on purpose, right? But he'd never gone this long without sending messages before. In fact, he had never missed even once. Maybe she was wrong. So, she decided to give him one more chance.

> Hi, Edward, I hope you are okay. I'm a little worried that you haven't said anything since this morning. It's not like you. Please say something.

Kate waited for his response, but no reply came. After a while, she decided Edward was not going to say anything. Was he giving her the silent treatment? Had he decided she wasn't worth the effort anymore?

She tried to distract herself with another movie on Netflix, but she couldn't concentrate on the screen. Her mind was running wild in a world full of negative thoughts, and before she knew it, she was crying quietly.

She'd believed in him. She'd wanted to believe in everything he said. But all her doubts, fears, and suspicions were impossible to ignore. Something terrible could've happened to him, or he could have chosen to abandon her. She'd never know either way. That had been the whole point she'd tried to make to him: She would never know what to believe unless she saw him with her own eyes.

She let tears stream down her cheeks and didn't even bother to wipe them off. The movie had ended some time ago, but she didn't care to turn the TV off. She sat motionless on the sofa for a while. The refrigerator hummed quietly, and soft voices came from the TV. She couldn't tell how much time had passed before she finally shook herself out of her thoughts, wiped her tears, and turned off the TV.

She didn't know how to cope with this devastation by herself. She sent a few messages to her mother, Sara, and her other friends, but none of them replied. Kate felt truly alone, and finally, she buried her face in her hands and let herself sob.

There was one thing she could admit to herself in her loneliness and heartbreak. She loved Edward. His sweet words and critical words. His questions and answers. His funny stories and sad stories. She'd loved them all. *What am I gonna do now?*

Well… there was nothing *to* do. It was over. The thought

was as heartbreaking as it was freeing. She looked at her hands, then shook her head and straightened up. "Well, Kate, that's the end of that romance," she told herself. She laughed quietly. Was it even a romance? Looking back on it, she thought so. "It was nice while it lasted."

Eventually, she mustered her strength and got ready for bed. She checked her phone one last time, and found a late, missed call from Sara that she'd missed–probably while she'd been crying her eyes out. Kate sent her a short reply promising to call in the morning and, exhausted from her tears, fell asleep right away.

****

Edward was very frustrated, too. The network outage had struck without warning, affecting a huge part of Kuala Lumpur–Edward's office and home included. It had lasted for two full days already. There was nothing he could do but wait until the network was restored.

He was worried about Kate. Was she worried about him? No–more likely she was angry. She'd been expecting an answer from him about meeting in person, and he could only imagine what she thought when he hadn't shown up for their daily conversation. He wished he could call her, but it was against the rules. No phone calls, no FaceTime–nothing that might let the woman on the other end see or overhear something she shouldn't. Kate had asked him to FaceTime more than once, but every time she brought up the subject, Edward had to make a lame excuse. *Sorry, Kate, my camera's broken. Sorry, no, I haven't had a chance to get it fixed yet–gotta have my laptop. Sorry, my phone is old, it doesn't have it...* Edward couldn't blame her for her frustration. He was frustrated with himself too.

Since he couldn't talk to her, Edward put all his energy

into thinking about how he could bring up the subject of financial problems to Kate. Getting her money was long overdue, as they had been chatting for months. Edward should have said something two weeks ago, but he kept postponing it. *If I mention money, Kate would certainly think this whole thing is a scam. I know that. But if I don't, Aidan will get suspicious. Either way, I'll lose what we have.* And that just wasn't acceptable to Edward. He'd played it up for Aidan's benefit, but more and more, what he'd told Kate was true: He was falling for her. She was everything he'd ever imagined in a wife. If he lost her, he would never find another like her.

He would have to find a way to ask for money without making Kate suspect it was a scam. But how? Edward thought hard, but couldn't come up with a good solution.

With nothing to do in the office, Aidan had no choice but to let everyone go home. As soon as Edward stepped outside, he started sweating. Malaysia was still in the dry season, and the unbearable humidity seemed to increase day by day.

"The next country I live in must have low humidity," Edward muttered as he walked. "I'll go back to Iceland. Or maybe California."

It was only a joke, but as soon as he said it, a sudden thought occurred to him. What if... he really did try to go to California? He'd been planning to escape Malaysia–and Aidan–for a while, but he'd never managed to decide where to go once he fled the country. Iceland was too dangerous; Aidan would find him immediately. There were the nearby Asian countries, or even Australia, but Edward had no contacts in any of those places, and they were too close for comfort. Until now, he'd been debating Canada, but... what if he really did what Kate asked? What if he actually met her in person?

He wanted to. It was risky–Aidan knew he hated his job,

but if he suspected Edward liked Kate, it would probably be easy for him to use his resources and track her down. But the more he thought about it, the more Edward wanted to do it. She was his guiding light–the key to his new life.

As he thought about all the possibilities with Kate, he reached his house. When he opened the front door, he smelled something appealing, and his hungry stomach growled.

"Something smells awfully good!" Edward exclaimed when he stepped inside the house.

"Hey, Dad! I made your favorite, spaghetti with meatballs!" Henrik shouted from the kitchen.

"Really? Well thanks, son! What's the occasion?"

"Well, I've got good news. Let's eat!"

As Henrik brought two plates to the table, Edward grabbed two cans of beer from the fridge. They sat down at the table and toasted; Edward could see Henrik fidgeting with excitement.

"Toast! Cheers!" They clinked the cans and drank, then started devouring their pasta. Cooking was normally Edward's domain, but when it came to spaghetti with meatballs, Henrik excelled; his meatballs were juicy and well-seasoned, and he always added the perfect amount of freshly grated Parmesan on top.

Edward didn't want to stop eating for even a moment, but he forced himself to pause so he could compliment his son. "This is so good, I can easily have a second plate."

"Glad you like it, Dad!"

"So, what is the good news, huh? Did you meet a nice girl?"

"No, Dad. Not a girl. I've been accepted into three colleges: Two in Iceland and one in America."

"Wow, that's great news! Congrats! Let's celebrate–bring us more beers, will you?" Edward was so proud of his son. Henrik was a smart boy, but he showed no arrogance in his intelligence.

He was also sensitive and caring. Edward was grateful Henrik had grown up to be such a nice young man without his mother around. Before Henrik was born, Edward had dreamed they'd be a family. But that was before his mother had disappeared without a word. Edward had never gotten the courage to ask Aidan about what happened to her, and her disappearance was the one thing Aidan never held over his head.

"Which college in America?" Edward asked as they drank.

"Stanford University. Remember I told you I might apply there?"

"Yes, yes, I do remember. Where is Stanford again…?"

"Oh Dad." Henrik shook his head. "It's in California."

"Right, in California… California? California?!" Edward's eyes lit up.

SIX

"Well?" Sara put down her empty teacup. They'd missed each other's calls a few times, and eventually, Sara had simply invited herself over. Kate still felt emotionally fragile, but it was nice to have someone in the house. It reminded her that she wasn't alone. "What's happening with your online lover?"

"Who?" Kate reached for her teacup to refill it. "Oh, him? It's over," she said as nonchalantly as she could.

"Over? When did that happen?"

"Last night."

"What happened?"

"He decided to end it. That's all." Kate did her best to look and sound as though it was no big deal.

"He did? What did he say?"

"Well, he was supposed to make plans for us to meet in person. But he hasn't said anything for two full days, so I decided that he must've been a scammer after all."

Kate thought Sara would be relieved. But instead, her friend looked troubled. "Aren't you making a kind of hasty decision here? Don't get me wrong, I still think this whole thing is too good to be true. But if he's just been gone for a couple of days…"

Kate interrupted Sara.

"He has never missed sending me messages, not once since we started talking. Even when I didn't reply for a day or two, he kept it up. So, I think I made a reasonable decision."

"You could be right, but… what if he got really sick? Or maybe his power went out or something." Seeing Kate's troubled expression, she quickly added, "You know I don't trust him. But… I don't know. Are you sure you're not just giving up because you're scared of getting hurt?" She shrugged. "If I were you, I'd give it a little more time. See if you don't hear back from him. But it's up to you, Kate. I just want you to be safe and happy."

After Sara left, Kate thought over her words. Tentatively, she opened her Facebook. Then, she saw it: messages from Edward.

Good evening, Kate. Hope you are doing fine. I missed you so much...

Kate, are you there?

I'm so sorry that I couldn't send you any messages for the past couple of days. There was a huge network outage in London. It hit my work, my house...

We even lost some really important documents for work... it was horrible.

But I won't complain anymore. Are you busy? Can you reply soon? I thought about you the whole time.

Kate could hardly believe it. Sara had been right! Without thinking, she immediately replied.

> Edward? It's so nice to hear from you!

I'm so happy you're online! How have you been?

> Better now. But to be honest with you, I was really miserable for the last two days.

> I couldn't understand why you suddenly quit sending me messages. I thought you were trying to get out of meeting me. Or that you decided scamming me was too much effort in the end.

Kate, how many times have I asked you to trust me? I keep telling you I'm serious about you. It makes me sad that you still don't believe me.

> I'm sorry. I want to believe you and trust you, but...

But what?

> But I can't help it.

I'm not playing any games here.

Everything I have ever said is the truth. I
love you.

...I love you, too...

It was scary to type it out like that. To tell Edward her true
feelings. But she wanted to be honest with him too.

Oh Kate, you can't believe how much joy
that gives me!

I wish I could hold you right now.

Kate was crying again. All the bad feelings about him that
had built up over the past two days instantly dissipated. Kate
felt ecstatic and wished he were right beside her.

Kate, are you there? Can you say it
again?

No way! Only once.

Please say it once more! Please.

No.

Fine...
It's okay. I'm still so happy. I wish I could
touch you.

When we meet, I'm going to find out
exactly what turns you on. Wherever you

feel the most pleasure, that's where I
want to touch you first.

> Edward! You know I don't do
> sex talk online.

I know, sorry... I couldn't help it.
I do want to know, though.

> Stop.

Okay, okay.

Kate shook her head, pressing a hand to her cheek. She was blushing.

> Anyway, did you get that big
> contract?

What contract?

> The big one for your company.

For a minute, Edward didn't reply.

Oh, I should find out within a few days.

> Then, you still can't tell me
> when you will come see me?

No.

You were going to tell me a
few days ago, remember?

I know. I'm sorry. But the outage really
set us back. We're trying to catch up, but
it's hard.

Just wait for a few more days, and I
promise I'll tell you when I can leave
London.

Okay.

Kate looked at the clock. It was already midnight.

I'm afraid I should go now.
Good night, Edward.

Okay, good night, Kate. Sweet dreams
and dreams of us. I love you.

Kate stayed awake for a long time that night, reflecting on
her behavior. Edward made her feel like a teenage girl. Her
emotions were like a rollercoaster, going up and down. One
moment she was ecstatic, and the next, she was completely
wrecked. Last time she'd acted like this, she'd been in college,
dating Ken. They'd talked on the phone every single day for
hours. When he didn't call one day, she'd been convinced he
was no longer interested in her. Later, she found out that he'd
had trouble with his home phone. That had been long before
cell phones were common.

Kate let out a scoff. Twenty years later, she was still acting
like the same college girl. It was embarrassing, but admittedly,

it made a little sense. Her relationship with Edward reminded her so much of her relationship with Ken, after all. She was behaving exactly the same way with Edward because he made her feel just like Ken had. She loved Ken dearly; thus, she must love Edward deeply. This revelation surprised her, but it helped her understand why she behaved like a madwoman, her emotions yo-yoing all over the place.

Kate knew her friends and her colleagues viewed her as a logical person. Around them, she used her reasoning to solve all problems. But with a man whom she dearly loves, she always became an emotional fool. It didn't matter how calm and collected she was when she was giving others advice: When it was her turn, she lost all reason.

She thought of Ken for a minute, then thought of Edward. Their images overlapped in her mind. Ken had been Japanese, and Edward was Icelandic. But they were both funny, smart, and made Kate completely comfortable in their presence. The only difference between these two men was that she had been able to see Ken whenever she wanted, since they'd lived so close together; she couldn't do that with Edward.

Maybe, if Edward couldn't make it to California, she could go see him instead. With that idea floating in her mind, Kate finally yawned and fell asleep.

****

Edward had found answers to both of his questions: how to ask Kate for money in an unsuspicious way, and how to get out of Malaysia to start a new life with her. He had an idea, at least. Whether it would work or not was another story. He had to try, and the timing was critical.

Admittedly, though, he was dragging his feet. He'd been delighted to reconnect with her after the outage; as he'd expected, she had been angry, but her confession brought him great joy. It was all he'd been able to think about. He'd intended on waiting a few more days to bring up money anyway, but before he knew it, another week had already passed.

At the end of their conversation each day, Kate asked, *Do you know when you'll make it to California yet?* She'd even brought up the idea of coming to see him in London. He'd evaded giving her a straight answer, but he was running out of time. If he didn't give Kate an answer, she would feel hurt and grow suspicious again. But if he didn't ask her for money soon, Aidan would catch on.

This had never been a problem before. He simply read off his scripts. He'd never liked the work, but the women he spoke to were just strangers. Edward had only ever focused on protecting himself and his son. But with Kate, it was different. He truly loved her and didn't want to hurt her. He knew that Kate still doubted him, and he couldn't really blame her. After all, half of what he told her was a lie. He didn't live in London. He didn't own a company. He didn't have any big contract pending. He had not accomplished that much in his life. He never had a wife, and she certainly did not die four years ago. But everything else–his likes and dislikes, his thoughts and opinions about the world, his hopes and dreams–was true. None more so than his feelings for her.

How could he make her believe him and trust him? When he asked her for money, she would most certainly back off, thinking that the whole thing was a scam after all. She would be completely devastated. Even if his plan went perfectly and she found out the truth, there was a chance she would still never want to talk to him again. His efforts would be wasted. Edward sighed.

The door flew open, and Aidan burst in. He headed

straight for Edward's desk. As soon as he got close, he stood over Edward menacingly.

"Making any progress with that American chick? What is her name, anyway?"

"Kate," Edward said, a little defensively.

"When are you going to get money from her?"

Edward couldn't lie; Aidan could easily check his messages. In fact, he probably already knew, and only wanted a reason to come after him. "I haven't mentioned it yet…"

"What the fuck are you waiting for? It's been months!"

"Sorry, I… didn't want to scare her off." It wasn't the best answer, but at least it wasn't too suspicious. Aidan knew some women needed extra convincing. Quickly, Edward added, "But I'm going to today."

"Damn right you will. I'll come back and check later." With that, Aidan stormed out of the room.

Edward sighed again. Well, that took one choice out of his hands. Hating himself for what he had to do, he typed out his first message.

Hello, Kate. How was your day?

> Hello Edward, my day was good. How was your night?

My night was good, too. What are you doing right now? Have you had your dinner yet?

> I'm not doing anything, just chatting with you. No, I haven't eaten yet. Not hungry. Maybe I'll have a small bowl of soup later or something.

Not hungry? What happened?

Nothing. Just feeling a little
tired and...

...and lonely?

Yes, you read my mind.

Every night I wish you were
here with me...

I know, Kate. I feel the same way and
more.

Edward stared at his screen and took a deep breath.

Kate, I have some good news and not-
so-good news. The good news is that the
contract I have been working on is
almost finalized. It just needs one final
thing.
 The bad news is that I won't be able
to come see you for at least another
month.

Another month?! Why?

Is it still because of this
contract? What else do you need?

I know, I'm sorry, but I just cannot leave
the country until this goes through.

Everything depends on this or I would've walked away from them months ago.

What I need is... I don't know how to bring this up, so I'm just gonna say it.

My company doesn't have the full funds. I've tried and tried to negotiate, but I'm still $5,000 short. I don't know what else I can do.

You need $5,000 to complete a contract?

That doesn't make sense...

It's an investment thing. It's kind of complicated, but basically, I have to invest some funds before my company can receive profits in return.

I won't bore you with the details. But the fact is, if I can't find another $5,000, everyone at my company is screwed.

Edward waited. Kate didn't say anything, so, reluctantly, he continued.

The only thing left is to pay from my own pocket. But honestly, I don't have that kind of money. It's embarrassing, but our profits are really low. Everything I make, I've saved for my son's college fund.

I thought about asking some family and friends for help, but they already gave me money when I first opened this company. So I don't want to do that to them again.

Kate... I want to meet you so badly. But I think the only way that's possible is... if you could lend me the money.

I know how this looks to you. But I don't have anyone else to turn to.

SEVEN

R omance scammers, who are typically male, confess their love in a relatively short period of time...

...certain the woman has fallen in love with him, he starts talking about financial problems. Common excuses are medical bills, business troubles, and...

...usually ask for between $3,000 and $5,000...

Kate Fleming, you are a fool.

A new day broke in California. Early morning birds chirped noisily as usual, and warm sunshine shined through the curtains. It was still early in the morning, but Kate woke up quietly. It was only 6:00 am; she didn't even have to turn off her alarm on the phone, which was set for 7:00 am. She sat up on her bed and stayed there for some time. Her eyes hurt from crying herself to sleep. All she wanted was a nap.

Kate? Are you there? Kate, please don't
disappear on me. I really need your help.

Kate shook Edward's last messages out of her head. She went to the bathroom to brush her teeth, then she took a shower. The warm water seemed to soothe her pain a little. She wished she could just stay in the shower forever, feeling the warm water on her wounded body and soul.

She'd really fallen in love with a scammer. That was the unavoidable truth. Sara, Dominique, even her own mother had warned her about the exact scenario she found herself in now. Of course they had. It was obvious from the start that it was a scam. Kate was the one who had ignored the doubts in her mind. She had believed him and loved him. Now, all she wanted to do was hide.

As she dressed comfortably, her stomach reminded her that she'd skipped dinner. Edward's messages had numbed her, and she'd immediately curled up in bed and cried herself to sleep like a child. She normally ate only a bowl of oatmeal and fruit, but this morning, she needed an excuse to stay away from her messages. Kate boiled a couple of eggs, cut some fruit, and even made herself some whole wheat pancakes. By the time she placed all the food on the table, she could turn on the TV to catch the 7:00 news. She ate and watched for a while without thinking about anything. Only the sound of the front door opening drew her attention.

"Good morning, Kate. Are you up?" Miki called.

"Mom? You're up very early. What happened?"

"Nothing. Just paying an early morning visit to my favorite daughter," Miki chuckled, walking toward the dining table. Kate mustered up a smile.

"Your favorite daughter, huh? I'm the only daughter you have, Mom."

"Oh, that's right, haha. I see you already had your breakfast. I brought you some croissants and scones. Fresh out of the oven!"

"Thanks, mom. I'll take one." Kate reached out and grabbed a croissant. Miki was right, it was nice and warm in her hand.

"You seem to have a big appetite this morning," Miki said, sitting down.

"Yeah, I didn't eat dinner last night, so I was hungry when I woke up."

"No dinner? How unusual. Did something happen last night?"

Kate stood up. "Mom, do you want some pancakes and a soft-boiled egg?"

"Yes, that sounds good."

Kate went into the kitchen and grabbed some pancakes and one soft-boiled egg. When she returned to the table with the plate, Miki asked the same question without missing a beat. "Did something happen last night?"

She really couldn't get anything past her mother. "Oh, nothing. I just ended things with Edward. That's all," Kate said as if it was nothing.

"Why? I thought it was going well." Miki looked puzzled.

"Yeah, it was going well, but ..."

"But what? What happened?"

Kate forced herself to look calm. "He asked me to send him some money. That's what happened."

"He did? Oh no... so you think you got scammed?"

"What else could it be? He tried to scam me. The whole thing was nothing but a lie..."

"Oh, Kate...I'm so sorry..." Miki was clearly at a loss for words. Soon she recovered from the initial shock and said, "Oh well, it's good that you found out now, before it was too late. Right?"

Kate shook her head. "It's too late. I was already in love with him. I didn't give him my money, but he took my heart away. He stole it from me..." Kate couldn't keep her calm composure any longer. The numb, calm sadness she'd felt all morning gave way to heartbreak and sorrow, and she couldn't stop her tears. Miki got up, walked to Kate, and hugged her tightly. Neither moved for a long time.

****

He'd known it was coming, but Edward couldn't help worrying.

He knew that Kate was upset and confused. More importantly, she was hurt. But there was nothing Edward could do to comfort her. All he could do was keep sending his messages to keep Aidan off his back. He tried to comfort himself; it was inevitable, after all, that he ask Kate for money. If he hadn't done it, Aidan would question him, and that was the last thing Edward needed. He couldn't have Aidan suspect anything until he was long gone, hopefully on his way to Kate. Until then, Edward had to keep working, following all the rules, just like he had done for the past twenty years.

Aidan came back later that day to check Edward's messages, as he'd said he would. When Aidan saw them, he was satisfied. That, at least, was a relief–but only a minor one. Edward knew that the next time Aidan bothered him, it would be to see if he'd received the money. How long would Edward have? Two weeks? A whole month? Who knew? It all depended on Aidan's mood.

Edward knew one thing for certain, though. Aidan wouldn't tolerate failure, not after Edward had spent so long on Kate and only Kate, lying about needing time to convince her. If Edward was still stuck as his employee when Aidan finally lost his patience…

…No. Edward's plan had to succeed. There was no other alternative.

****

Kate couldn't concentrate on her work. Her thoughts kept going back to one word, "money." When she and Edward had stopped talking in the past, it had only lasted for a day or two, and was usually only because of misunderstandings or small disagreements. When they resumed their conversation, they could continue as if nothing had happened. But the situation was completely different this time.

There was no misunderstanding. The hard fact was that Edward was a scammer. There was no question about it.

Though talking to her mother had helped, Kate's thoughts were still in disarray. At last, she gave up trying to focus on work. She was days ahead of schedule on her project anyway–she could afford a day off. She grabbed her phone and, after a moment of contemplation, decided to call Sara. Kate never knew whether Sara would answer or not; luckily, this time, she picked up.

"Hi Kate, what's up?"

"Hi Sara." It was tempting to say she was fine, but she decided to be honest. "I'm… not so good. Can we get coffee?"

"Sure, I'll meet you at that café downtown. Half an hour?"

"Okay, see you in a bit."

Kate quickly changed her clothes and put on a little makeup. The café, one that she and Sara used to frequent, was easy to get to from her house, and traffic was light. When she arrived, Sara was already there waiting. As soon as she saw Kate, she waved.

"Sorry I'm a bit late," Kate was breathing a bit fast, as she ran up to meet Sara.

"No problem. I got here early since there was no traffic. So what's going on, huh?"

"Let's get a seat, and I'll tell you everything."

They chose a seat in the back of the café with no one in

the vicinity. After the waitress brought their drinks, Kate sipped her coffee and began to recount what happened the night before. Surprisingly, Kate felt calm as she talked. Explaining it all to Sara felt like telling someone else's story. Sara listened attentively, saying nothing until Kate finished talking. Then she growled, "That jerk. Gosh, I'm so sorry, Kate. I really didn't want to be right. I'd hoped you guys could work things out."

"Yeah, me too. You know, I loved him…" Kate said, looking into the distance. "I poured all my energy into talking to him. You know we talked every day? For more than two months. We talked about our pasts and our future together. I thought he was so funny, considerate and caring. He said he loved me and will love me for the rest of his life. He was going to come see me in a month." She tightened her grip on her coffee cup. "But it was all a lie, nothing but a lie. I was so naïve."

The two women were quiet for a while. Eventually, Kate continued, "But you know what? I got one good thing out of this mess. I know I can still fall in love with someone after all these years of no love life."

"That's great, Kate! I'm glad for you. Really." Sara tapped her nails on the table, looking thoughtful. "I've got an idea! Why don't we go somewhere for a week or two?"

"Go somewhere?"

"Yeah! Let's travel somewhere, get far away from here. A change of scenery will do you good, and we haven't really spent time together in ages."

Kate felt a pang of guilt. She opened her mouth to apologize, but Sara held up her hand. "Don't, it's not your fault. We've all just gotten busy over the years. But you deserve a break, and honestly, so do I. Otherwise I'll track down this guy and beat him up for you." Kate laughed, and Sara smiled, looking pleased. "There, I'm glad to see you happy. Hey, I'm gonna ask Jane and Mary, too. We can have some fun, all four of us!"

Now that Kate thought about it, she hadn't taken any vacations in over a year. "You know, I always wanted to visit Southeast Asia, like Thailand or Malaysia." The more she thought about it, the more excited she felt. "Oh, or Cambodia. They've got that–what was it called, Angkor Wat? That big temple. I've always wanted to go see it."

"Sounds good. I'll make all the arrangements," Sara promised, equally enthusiastic.

Eventually, they parted ways with a promise to finalize their plans soon. When Kate returned home, she realized she felt much better. Her focus and motivation had returned. Turns out, you really should have just spent time with your friends after all.

Kate worked until six, when her phone rang. It was Dominique.

"Hi Mom. Sorry about what happened with Edward."

"Thanks. But how did you know that?"

"Grandma called me and told me all about it. I can't believe it was a scam after all."

"I know. Oh well, *c'est la vie*, huh?" Kate didn't want to dwell on it, not when she was finally feeling better. "Hey, I might go away for a week or so with my friends."

"Where are you going?"

"Southeast Asia."

"Really? How nice! Yeah, go have some fun. It'll do you some good." Kate smiled. Dominique sounded just like Sara.

"How's Tren?"

"He's good. He's here, actually, he says hi."

"Really! Say hi to him, too."

After they hung up, Kate made a small salad, then went

back to her office. As she ate, she began to research Southeast Asia, opening tab after tab of tourist-centered websites. As she glanced through them, she realized she'd forgotten to close the Facebook tab. She could have closed it without looking, but she hesitated, and curiosity won out.

Hi Kate, how are you? You haven't said anything since last night, so I'm getting worried. Can you please tell me what's going on?

Kate, are you there? Why are you not saying anything? You know I don't like the silent treatment. Please talk to me... Kate, are you there?

With every message, Kate's anger grew. How dare he ask what was going on? She wanted to say something, but she resisted the urge to reply to him. Instead, she closed out of the account entirely.

It wasn't yet dark outside, and as she moved through the house, the garden caught her eye. Finally, her flowers were in full bloom, and the yard looked and smelled amazing. She stepped outside to cut some, enough to fill a nice vase, which she placed in the center of her dining table. She hadn't realized how dreary the dining room looked without a little color, and the sight of the flowers cheered her immensely. Though they wouldn't last long, it was worth it.

After a shower, she settled down on her bed to read a book. Her phone rang again: It was Sara. Kate answered without a preamble.

"Hi Sara, thanks for the coffee this afternoon."

"You're welcome. Guess what? My travel agent just called me and said we're all set. I love him, he's so efficient. We are leaving in a week for ten days of adventure in Southeast Asia. How does that sound?"

"Wonderful! Thanks, Sara! I'm so excited." Kate meant it, too. She could hear it in her own voice.

"Yeah, me too. I talked to Mary and Jane after I left this afternoon, and they're all in, too. I'm gonna call them and let them know we're all set."

"Good idea. Thanks again for everything, Sara!"

"That's what friends are for! Ciao!"

As she thought of her approaching freedom, Kate felt something lift inside of her. She was still heartbroken, she knew. Even now, she felt guilty for ignoring Edward's messages. Part of her wanted to run back even now and beg him to tell her that he wasn't scamming her. But she was smarter than that. And more importantly, Edward's betrayal was a gift in disguise. Just a few months ago, she'd felt dried up, stagnant, and old. He'd proved to her that she still had passion left in her body and mind, and she wasn't going to forget it again so easily.

What was it mom said? A "shriveled old husk"? Not likely!

Who needed Edward? Maybe she would even meet someone in Asia and fall in love. That, she thought, would be nice.

EIGHT

Hi Kate, how are you? Hope you're fine. I miss you so much, my whole body aches with it. I miss your words and your jokes. Please say something.

Hi Kate, how are you doing? Hope your day was good. I dreamed of us last night. It was really nice. I got to hold you and kiss you...

Anyway, I have good news about my son. He's leaving for a college in Iceland. I'm so proud of him. I'm sure he'll love college life over there.

Another lie. Edward was so fed up with lies. He couldn't even tell Kate where Henrik was truly going to school: not Iceland, but Stanford, in California. So, so close to where Kate was.

But Edward couldn't tell the truth, because Aidan might see it. If Aidan saw it, then it was the end of the plan Edward had been nurturing. He couldn't afford to blow his cover, not when he was so close to putting this last-ditch escape effort into action. He had to make sure that everything was business as usual. He would have to pretend to be a good worker until he got out of this place. *Stay here just a little bit longer…just a little bit longer…*

Those words had become his mantra over the years. They reminded him of his father's favorite song–a Jackson Browne classic that he'd listened to on repeat when Edward was a child. Nowadays, he clung to them as a reminder to keep going even when all felt hopeless.

He sighed as he looked at his computer screen. A row of his own messages stared back at him, unanswered. He knew, of course, why Kate hadn't said anything. She'd never made a secret of her suspicions about him, and unfortunately, she was right. But he had to ask her, again and again. Anything to stop Aidan from growing suspicious.

Hey Kate, hope everything is okay with you. I'm worried and I miss you so much.

Still wondering if you could help me with my financial problem. I really need that money to pay the investor and close the deal. If I wait too long, I might miss the opportunity.

Of course I'd pay you back once we started making a profit. I'd never take advantage of you. I know it's hard to believe, but I hope you can trust me.

It's okay that you need to think about it, but let me know soon, please?

How many times had Edward typed those words over the

past twenty years? Too many to count. He just followed the script that was given to him and did not think twice. He tried as hard as he could not to think about how he'd ended up in this awful position. But at times like these, he couldn't stop the memories from creeping in.

Eighteen years old and fresh out of high school, he'd decided to take a gap year. His parents, who were both still working high-paying jobs at the time, had agreed to let him travel before he started college. Gap years weren't uncommon—people wanted work experience, or just to enjoy their last bit of freedom before becoming true adults. Edward had wanted to see the world.

He'd started with the Scandinavian countries. From there, he made his way to western Europe, meandering through England, France, Spain, and Italy. He'd even dipped his toes into central Europe, like Poland and the Czech Republic. For five months, he enjoyed food, landmarks, art, and people, then headed home.

If he could've done it all over again, he would've ended his journey there. He would have forgone his last few months of freedom and stayed safely at home. But that wasn't what happened.

One day, when he was watching some documentary on TV, he saw Angkor Wat, the largest temple in the world. He'd never heard of it before, and he was instantly fascinated. As he hunted for more information, he learned more and more about Cambodia's neighboring countries—Thailand, Vietnam. Malaysia. He decided that his final gap year adventure, before starting life as a college student, would be traveling through Southeast Asia.

Naturally, he first went to Cambodia to see Angkor Wat. It was exactly how he'd imagined and more. He felt an indescribable awe standing in front of it—the kind of awe one only felt when standing in front of something so beautiful, so spectacular. Edward felt as if his whole body was enchanted by the magic power the temple emitted, and he stood still for a long time, just gazing at it in wonder. The visit went off without a hitch; he still had mementos from his time there. Thailand and Vietnam were equally interesting. Both countries had long, fascinating histories, and they each had a different ambience.

At last, he ended up in Malaysia. He'd only stayed in each country for a few days, and that had been the plan for Kuala Lumpur, too. On his last full day, he stopped by a bar. His flight was not until the next evening, so he decided to grab a beer and try chatting with the locals. As he stepped into the bar, he realized that he was the only white person there—the only foreigner at all, for that matter. He had no idea that he was on Aidan's territory. He hadn't even known who Aidan was.

Everyone's eyes were glued on him, but after so much time traveling, Edward had grown used to it. He'd never been able to shake off that "tourist" appearance, but he'd wanted to seem friendly and approachable. When a man approached and asked if he was up for a challenge, he thought he had succeeded, and happily agreed. Edward thought the man was his opponent, but it turned out to be a girl sitting a few tables away. They introduced themselves, and Edward took a seat.

When it came to drinking contests, Edward was certain he would win. The girl—Jana, she'd said—was so small compared to him, after all. They clinked shot glasses, and the contest began. They matched the first shot, then the second. a third, fourth, fifth. Edward's head began to spin. Jana didn't seem affected at all. She simply poured another round, encouraging him to keep going. Stubborn pride carried him through the sixth, seventh, eighth, ninth, and tenth shot. By this time,

Edward was completely wasted. He barely recognized who he was talking to, and he certainly couldn't understand what they were saying. But the drinking contest continued. He matched Jana for five more shots before he blacked out completely.

The next morning, Edward found himself in an unfamiliar place. As he woke up, he saw Jana sleeping next to him. How did he end up sleeping in her bed? He remembered nothing, nothing at all. And that was where Aidan came in.

Hey Kate. I'm thinking about you again.
I was really hoping to hear back from you
by now.

Kate, I'm begging you. Please think
about it. The sooner I get this money, the
sooner we can meet like you want.

Asking for money always troubled Edward. With Kate, it was much harder. But she would understand that he had to protect Henrik. He just had to make sure she was willing to listen.

Henrik would leave for California in a little over a week. School didn't begin until September, but he'd said he'd saved up enough money to travel around the U.S. before settling down for college. Just like his dad—though Henrik, of course, had no idea what had actually happened to Edward, and Edward made sure Henrik would never copy his mistakes.

With Henrik going to California, Edward was very hopeful. He was going to ask him a small favor at the airport. Everything had to be done right, and timing was crucial. Otherwise, his plan would not work. Until then, Edward had to play his part.

Hi Kate, how are you? I'm thinking about
you again...

****

The trip was only a few days away, and Kate still had so much to do before she left: finishing her work, getting her hair and nails done, shopping for new clothes and shoes, deciding what to pack, the list went on and on. Though she couldn't wipe Edward from her mind and heart so quickly, her travel preparations were enough to keep her distracted, and she was grateful.

On the morning of their departure, Kate did one last round of checks to make sure she had packed everything. Passport, checked. Phone, checked. Laptop– oh. Laptop not checked. She hurried to her office and found it on her desk, sitting with all her tabs and work still open.

"Can't believe I almost forgot you," she muttered to herself. As she leaned over to shut it off, her gaze fell on the list of open tabs. She hadn't checked Facebook since the day she'd closed the tab. Really, she knew she should've deleted the account entirely. But her heart wouldn't let go so easily, so she'd settled for refusing to check the site. Now, though, she couldn't resist the urge to look. It was just to confirm that Edward had moved on, she told herself, even though she knew deep down it was a lie. But she couldn't imagine he would have persisted with his messages for much longer after it became clear Kate was ignoring him. He knew very well she wouldn't send him a dime. In fact, it made her angry to realize he'd been bold enough to ask for her money anyway, even after she'd told him she suspected he was a scammer. He must've thought she was stupid.

As she opened the account, she was shocked to find many

messages from Edward. He hadn't missed even one day since she stopped chatting with him. He always concluded his messages saying that he loved her and missed her, but he also asked her about the money. He even said he knew she was probably suspicious, but he begged her for help anyway.

Did he... actually need the money? What if he was telling the truth? He obviously knew she would think he was lying. But he was asking so diligently anyway. It had to be a blow to his pride. But then again, there was no way Kate would send him money...

Kate stood there for a few minutes, lost in thought. Eventually, her phone rang; it was Sara. "Kate, where are you? I hope you're on your way."

"Um... I'm leaving now." Kate looked at the clock and was shocked to see how late it had gotten. "Oh my god, I'd better hurry."

"Yeah, you'd better. See you soon!"

When Kate arrived at the airport, Sara, Jane, and Mary were already there, looking anxious. Jane spotted her first and waved frantically. "Kate, what happened? It's not like you. You're always the first one anywhere." Mary nodded, her worried expression matching Jane's.

"Sorry guys. But I'm here. Let's get this thing rolling!" Luckily, the trip to the airport had given Kate enough time to clear her mind, and she led the way to the check-in counter with confidence. The four friends made it through check-in and security with ease; they still had a little time to spare once they reached their gate, so they sat down in chairs near the window.

"I'm so excited about this trip. I've been wanting to go to Thailand for a long time," Sara said.

"Me, too," Kate agreed.

Sara looked at her thoughtfully. Mary and Jane were going

through a travel brochure and chatting with each other, not paying attention. "Are you sure you're okay?" she asked.

"Yeah, I'm okay. Why do you ask?"

"Because you look a little worried."

"What? Me? No, I'm not worried about anything." Kate tried to look high-spirited, though under Sara's scrutiny, it felt forced.

"Okay, if you say so… but if you want to tell me something, I'm always all ears, okay?"

"Got it. Thanks, Sara. You are the best."

The boarding announcement rang out, and the four women stood up and joined the long line. As Mary, Jane, and Sara talked about what they would do once they arrived in Thailand, Kate looked at their plane parked outside the window, lost in her thoughts. Jane showed her boarding pass, followed by Mary, Sara, and finally Kate. Together, they headed down the walkway and boarded the airplane.

****

"Hey Henrik, are you home? Edward shouted as he opened the front door. He pulled a brand-new suitcase into the house behind him.

"Yeah, dad. I'm right here." Henrik ran down the stairs to meet Edward in the living room.

"Son, I've picked up your plane ticket and a new suitcase." Edward pushed the suitcase toward Henrik and spun it. Henrik took it, grinning.

"Thanks! I was thinking about getting a new one, 'cause I wasn't sure if my old one was big enough to pack everything I need. Man, I can't believe I'll be living in California in a week!"

Edward smiled. It was nice to see Henrik so excited. He was due to depart in a few days, and they'd been busy getting ready. Since Edward couldn't accompany him, he wanted to make sure that Henrik had everything he needed. If Henrik thought he was being overbearing, he graciously didn't mention it.

"Henrik, have you made a list of things to pack?"

"Yeah, dad. I have it right here."

"Let me see."

Henrik pulled the list out of his pocket and handed it over. Edward examined it carefully and said, "Looks like this is everything you need. But if you come up with something else, just add it here, okay? I'll take care of packing for you."

"Yeah, I'll do that. Thanks, dad."

"Good."

Edward willed himself to be calm. It was time to start putting his plan in motion. He said, "Son, I need to tell you a few things. They're very important, so listen very carefully and keep them in your head. Don't write them down anywhere, okay?"

"What is it, Dad?"

"Let's sit down here…" He guided his son over to the couch, and they both took a seat. "Well…" Edward cleared his throat. "First of all, I'm so proud that you got into Stanford and you have my full support. Just ask me whenever you need anything, anything at all. But I need you to do a few things for me. First, you'll be flying into Iceland."

"What?! Why? I'm going to California!"

"I know. Please just let me finish. Then you can ask me all the questions–actually, I take it back. Please don't ask any questions. I promise I'll tell you everything when the time comes, but the less you know right now, the better."

Henrik looked confused, and Edward couldn't blame him. His son had never seen him like this before. He wished he could explain everything, but he couldn't take that risk. "So, you'll be flying into Iceland and staying with your grandparents for a little while. From there, I want you to buy a one-way ticket to San Francisco and eight postcards. Don't worry, I'll send you the money. Fill out the postcards–it doesn't matter what they say, just something generic–and give them to your grandma. Tell her to mail two per year: one for me and the other for your uncle Aidan. That should cover the next four years." Of course, if Edward successfully managed to escape Malaysia, he would tell his parents not to do that. But he needed a backup plan to protect Henrik, just in case. "Uncle Aidan thinks you will be a freshman at Reykjavik University. We need him to believe that for as long as possible. You got that?"

Edward spoke fast, trying to get everything out as quickly as he could. Logically, he knew he was being paranoid–even Aidan wasn't crazy enough to wire-tap his house–but he couldn't help it. Henrik looked confused, but did not say anything, simply staring at his father. Edward could read all the questions in his expression, but Henrik didn't ask any of them. He just nodded slowly.

"Henrik, thanks for not saying anything. I really appreciate it," said Edward, almost in tears. It all came down to this: timing, luck, and faith in love.

The days passed very quickly. Everyday there was something new to do: picking up Henrik's renewed passport, paying tuition and housing, purchasing new clothes. Edward had never planned to go to an American school, so the process was entirely new; on top of all that, he had to be careful how he moved his money, so as not to draw Aidan's attention. Luckily, after so many years under his thumb, Aidan had stopped exerting quite so much control over him. It was unlikely that he was looking as closely as Edward feared he was. He would obviously make sure that Edward didn't try to jump on a plane with Henrik, but otherwise, Edward suspected Aidan thought he'd given up trying to get away in order to keep Henrik safe.

In truth, Edward didn't think Aidan would ever actually hurt Henrik directly. Aidan had never told Henrik the truth of why Edward worked for him, or even anything about his scam company. In fact, he doted on Henrik, so much that Edward wondered if Aidan viewed Henrik as his own son. But even if Aidan loved Henrik, Edward wanted Henrik far away from him. Henrik didn't need to get wrapped up in corruption like his father.

But most of all, Edward wanted to spend as much time as he possibly could with Henrik, as he wasn't sure when he could see his son again. If they were lucky, Edward would join him in California in just a few short months. But now, all Edward could do was hope.

The night before Henrik's departure, they stood in Henrik's room and checked everything one last time.

"You think you've packed everything?" Edward looked at Henrik.

"Um, I think so. Making a list was a great idea, Dad. I'm sure we would've missed a lot of stuff otherwise. And thanks again for helping me."

"Of course. This is going to be one of the biggest adventures of your life, so I wanted to do everything right."

"Dad, when are you going to come visit me in California?"

"Oh, I don't know, son. Soon, I hope. But remember, don't tell anyone that you're leaving for California. Everybody thinks you are going to a university in Reykjavik."

Henrik had to be sick of him saying that over and over, but he took it in stride.

"Got it, Dad. I won't say anything to anyone. But please come visit me soon, okay? Promise?"

"I promise."

They hugged each other for a long time. After Henrik went to bed, Edward went back to the office and sent Kate his daily message. He was lucky that Aidan was so fond of Henrik, because he'd cut Edward some slack about Kate's lack of responses. Any other time, and Edward never could've gotten away with failing to get money for so long. Edward was already prepared to face his wrath once Henrik was out of the country.

Kate, how are you? I wonder what you're up to these days.

Oh yeah, my son is leaving tomorrow for Iceland. Remember I said he was going to university there? I'll miss him so much...

I miss you very much. It's been almost two weeks since I heard from you. Please write to me. You know I don't like silence... and we can talk about the money, right?

I love you.

The next morning Edward and Henrik took an Uber to the airport. When they arrived at the security checkpoint, they saw Aidan and a few men waiting there. Aidan was shouting at them as usual, but when he spotted Edward and Henrik, he impatiently waved them over.

"What took you so long? He's gonna miss his plane!" Even in front of Henrik, Aidan couldn't help but yell at Edward and put him down. But Aidan was like that with most people, so Henrik had never seemed to find it weird. "Henrik, I'm gonna miss you, man. You take care of yourself, okay?" Aidan was almost in tears. No matter how often Edward saw him around Henrik, he could never quite believe the change in his attitude.

"I will, uncle Aidan. Thanks for everything. And for the money," Henrik said, looking grateful. After all, Henrik believed he was a real uncle. Every year, Aidan gave him money on his birthday and on New Year's. This time, he'd give him a substantial amount, telling him to enjoy his college years while he was still young. In a twisted way, Edward was grateful. Even if Aidan was nothing but a bully to him, he did, at the very least, pretend to be a good guy around Henrik.

"Oh, that's nothing. Wish I could give you more, but you know, how things are right now with my company…"

Edward spoke up. "Yeah, I want to thank you, too. Henrik told me about the money you gave him for the college."

"Oh, cut it out. Henrik, are you hungry? Thirsty? It's a long flight, you'll need a snack. I'll grab you something." With that Aidan was already running off, even before Henrik could say something.

"He loves you, you know?" Edward said, shaking his head.

"I know," Henrik said, looking in the direction Aidan went. Edward put a hand on his shoulder to draw his attention. The snack kiosk was close by; he only had time for a quick reminder.

"Make sure he gets those postcards every year for the next four years," he said, quickly and quietly. Henrik nodded, but before he could reply, Aidan was already back with the sandwich and a can of Coke.

"Here, Henrik, eat your sandwich."

"Thanks, uncle Aidan."

An awkward silence fell as Henrik ate. Aidan was hovering anxiously; he looked for all the world like his own child was going off to college. Not for the first time, Edward wondered why Aidan hadn't claimed Henrik as his own son. Some long-lost sense of self-awareness, maybe? Or maybe Edward was being too charitable.

When Henrik finished eating, it was time to go. He gestured toward the security line. "I'd better get inside…"

"Yeah, you'd better," Edward urged.

Henrik hugged Aidan and shook hands with Aidan's men, then faced his father. He'd been brave and excited the whole time they'd been preparing, but now, Edward could see tears in his eyes.

"Dad, I will miss you."

"I will miss you more, son." Edward pulled him in and hugged him tightly. He held on for a long time, reluctant to let him go. But there was one last thing Henrik needed to know, and Edward only had a few seconds to say it. Urgently, he whispered, "I put a letter in your suitcase. It's for Kate Fleming. She lives near Stanford, I think. Find her and give it to her as soon as you can."

Henrik looked puzzled, but said yes.

Edward and Aidan watched Henrik go through the security line and disappear into the terminal. They were silent for a while. Aidan spoke first.

"Well, he's gone. Now get back to work!" With that, Aidan turned and started walking. Edward was still watching the direction Henrik had gone. "Hey, Edward, get your ass moving!"

Edward reluctantly turned and started following the men. Aidan ran back and pushed him to hurry. Edward knew Aidan wouldn't leave the terminal until he made sure that Edward was in the car with him and was on his way back to the office. He motioned to the other men, who fell in step behind the two of them, making sure Edward couldn't turn around or try to slip away through the crowds. There were many people at the terminal and soon they were all nothing but a part of the crowd.

****

Kate sipped her coffee and relaxed against the chair in the airport café. Sara, Jane, and Mary were all caught up in conversation, looking through the photos from their trip. In an hour, they would board the plane back to California.

It had been an incredible vacation. Kate had decided to turn off her message notifications–especially ones from Facebook–so that she could enjoy her time with her friends and focus on the trip. In Thailand, they'd visited the opulent Grand Palace and its sacred Wat Phra Kaew Temple. They went on a night cruise on the boat-filled Chao Phraya River. There Kate met a French couple her age, and they hit it off right away. They spoke French to each other on the cruise, and when they exited the boat, they asked Kate if they could exchange email addresses, to which she happily obliged.

On their fourth day there, they rented a car and drove along the coastline. They only stopped once to eat lunch at the beach, taking in the white sand and beautiful blue water.

They left Bangkok early in the morning and did not get into Phnom Penh until late at night. By the time they checked into their hotel, they were exhausted. But they'd visited the incredible Angkor Wat, just like Kate wanted. If it had been up to her, they would've stayed for the rest of their vacation. They even spent that night in a nearby hotel, and they'd found a local restaurant to order breakfast from before they drove back to Phnom Penh. After visiting the ornate Royal Palace, the National Museum, and Choeung Ek–the infamous killing fields of Khmer Rouge–they headed to the airport to catch a plane to their last destination: Malaysia.

They'd made a lot of grand plans for Malaysia, but by the

time they arrived, they were exhausted. In Kuala Lumpur, they decided to take it easy and visited only two places–the famous Petronas Twin Towers and a UNESCO World Heritage Site, George Town. Kate immediately fell in love with George Town, the older part of Malaysia. She particularly liked its architecture and the ambience. She always preferred the old town to a modern section in any city in the world.

They spent most of their last two vacation days walking down the boulevards and shopping. They all agreed that ten days were not nearly enough to see all the things these countries had to offer. When they came back, they'd make time for Vietnam and Singapore too. Kate hadn't been so excited about traveling in a long time. In a way, she was grateful to Edward for that, too. If not for him, she wouldn't have rediscovered her passion for seeing the world.

As they heard the boarding announcement, they got up to leave. After a few steps, Kate stopped dead in her tracks. Sara caught Kate's reaction and asked, "Hey, Kate. What are you looking at?"

"I thought I saw Edward," Kate said, puzzled.

"Edward? You don't say. I thought he lived in London."

"Yes, he is in London. So, it can't be him…" He'd been on her mind all throughout the trip, but… was she really so pathetic that she was imagining things? She was heartbroken over him, but she didn't think she was that far gone. "I must've mistaken someone for him… But he really looked like Edward…"

Sara shrugged. "Hunh. Weird coincidence."

With that, the two women hurried to catch up with the other two, who were a few feet away. The four headed to their gate to board their plane back to California.

NINE

When Kate got home from the airport, she found her mother in the kitchen, cooking something.

"Hi Mom, I'm back. Something smells so good, what are you cooking?"

"Welcome home! I've cooked your favorite, the eel."

"Wow, thanks Mom! I'm gonna freshen up a bit and come right down." Kate headed upstairs with her suitcase. After a little while, she came down to join her mother in the kitchen.

"How was your trip?" Miki asked.

"It was wonderful! But I don't think I'll ever get used to the foods in that region. Very spicy. So, this eel is heavenly!"

"Hahaha, let's eat. Tell me all about your trip!"

Kate and Miki sat down at the counter. As they ate eels with rice, miso soup, and cucumber salad, Kate told Miki all about the countries they'd visited and everything she and the others had done while they were there. Miki loved traveling just as much as Kate did; she asked question after question, and Kate answered everything to her best knowledge.

"Sounds like you guys had kind of a hectic time there," Miki said after Kate finished a story about a wrong turn they'd taken in Cambodia.

"Yeah, but it was worth it. The girls all agreed that we would go back there soon. There's so much to discover in that region. And the history's so interesting."

"I know you liked world history in school. It was always your favorite subject. You liked geography too. You even memorized all the capitals in the world in the fifth grade, remember?"

"Yep, I think I still remember a lot of them."

Miki left after lunch, saying that she was meeting her friend downtown. Kate was tired from the long trip home, so she decided to take a nap. As she started up the stairs, something clicked in her mind. Edward.

She had not replied to any of his messages since he'd first asked for money. She also hadn't checked any of her messages while she was on vacation. It was easier with the girls around, but now that she was back home, alone, she could feel her heart urging her to see what else he might've said. Entering her bedroom, she opened her suitcase and took out her laptop. She sat on her bed and turned it on, then opened Facebook.

Just as she expected, there were many messages from him. He never missed even one day. She took time and read all of them. In every message, he made sure to tell her that he loved her and missed her. She sat there for a long time with the laptop on her lap, pondering whether she should say something, but in the end, her fatigue won. She laid down on her bed and fell fast asleep.

A familiar *ping* woke her. She immediately looked at her phone, but there was nothing on the home page. *Right, I turned off notifications.* She noticed it was six in the evening, much later than it had been. *I must've slept for a couple of hours. I thought I heard a ping, but that must've been in my dream.*

She'd left the laptop next to her on the bed; when she

opened it, she saw a new message from Edward.

Hi Kate. Hope you're doing well. You still haven't said anything but I'm patiently hoping to hear from you.

My son is gone, and I miss him dearly. But I miss you more, to tell you the truth.

I don't know what you did to me, but I don't think I can function without you. I keep thinking about meeting you someday, and that is the only thing that keeps me moving forward. I wish I could have gone to meet you when you first asked.

I miss talking to you every day. I really could've used your advice before my son left. You would've known the perfect things to say to encourage him. But me...

Never mind.

Say something, dear, pour moi, won't you? At least let me know you're reading these. Even if you refuse to send me any money, I just need to know that you're there.

Sending much love and kisses from London. I love you.

Kate read his messages repeatedly. She could feel her emotions welling up in her heart all over again, as if his attempt to scam her had never happened at all. She wanted, so badly, to believe that he truly cared for her and loved her dearly, the way she loved him. She wanted to be with him and share many moments together. She missed him so much. In fact, not even one day passed that she did not think of him. Even on her trip, she thought about him whenever she was by herself or when she saw a couple on the street. She wished that he were with her enjoying the trip.

She looked outside the window for a while, but she was not really paying attention to anything outside. Her mind was swirling. Then, she straightened up, determined.

> Hi Edward. I'm fine. How
> about you? Sorry that I haven't said
> anything for a long time. I was away for
> a little while. I miss you, too.

Kate! OMG

The reply came instantly, as if Edward had typed enthusiastically, without thinking. Kate couldn't help but smile.

Sorry. Hi Kate, it's okay. What matters is
that you're here now. You don't know
how happy this message makes me!
    You were away? Where did you go?

> My friends and I traveled to
> Southeast Asia.

Southeast Asia? Where did you go? Like,
which countries?

We visited Thailand,
Cambodia, and Malaysia in that order.
We love all three countries and want to
go back there soon. Have you been to
any of them?

You came t

Kate blinked at the partial message.

Sorry. I was sending a reply to my
business partner.

No, I have not been to any of those
countries. What made you choose
Southeast Asia?

My friends and I have gone to
Europe many times, so we wanted to go
somewhere we'd never been. Plus, we
always talked about going there one
day. So, we decided to make it happen.
It was a lot of fun!

Then, Kate remembered what she'd seen at the airport.
Edward would probably find it funny—or maybe even cute.

Oh yeah, guess what
happened at the Kuala Lumpur airport?

What happened?

We were having coffee at the
airport and just as we started heading
toward our gate, I saw a foreign man
being surrounded by several local men
and sort of escorted to the exit. And I
thought the man was you.

He really looked like you. I
mean, I've only seen the one photo of
you still, but...

See what thinking about you
every day does to me?

You saw me at the airport? When was
this?

A couple of days ago.

What date and what time?

Kate frowned, puzzled. Her heart began to beat faster.
Surely it hadn't really been him...?

Monday, June 3 around 3:30
PM...

Kate waited and waited, but Edward didn't reply for a long
time. Finally, she sent another message.

What is it, Edward?
...It wasn't actually you that I
saw, was it?

Finally, Edward responded.

Haha, that would have been a crazy
coincidence, huh?

Sorry, my love. Like I told you, I can't
leave London until this investment
contract is finalized.

Oh, okay.

Kate tried not to feel too disappointed. It was better this
way anyway–it meant he hadn't lied to her. Unless, of course,
he was lying to her now... but she pushed that thought away.
She was tired of doubting him.

So you haven't solved your
money problem yet?

No, not yet... but I'm still working on it.

We always talked about trust
and honesty, right? So, I want to be
honest with you.

I'm sorry to say this, but I
cannot send you any money.

It's not because I don't love
you. It's just against my rules.

Thanks for being honest with me. That's
what I like about you.

Let's talk about something else,
before you disappear again.

I won't disappear anymore.

You promise?

I promise.

And just like that, they fell back into easy conversation. It
was as if they'd never stopped talking, as if nothing had ever
thrown their relationship off-course.

Once, Kate read an online article about the phases of a
romantic relationship. To her, it seemed that the "romance
phase" of the relationship, during which time the man and the
woman fell in love, was now behind them. Most people assumed
that stability came after romance. But stability was actually the
third phase in the relationship. The second phase of the
relationship was called the 'Power Struggle' phase. All the love
that was lost or overshadowed by arguments and fights returned
as a matured love once the couple reached a point of stability.
After the struggle to try to change each other, they realized that
they just had to accept the way they were. Knowing that each
person was different, they could love each other with their good
points as well as their flaws.

Kate was glad that she'd distanced herself from Edward for
a while. It gave her the time and mental clarity to reaffirm her
love for him. As much as he said he loved her, Kate also dearly
loved him back. She missed him day and night. If that wasn't
love, what was it?

For the past few months, she had gone back and forth between logic and emotions like a yo-yo. She wrote Edward off as a scammer more than once, but every time she did so, she realized that there was some kind of force inside her that pulled her right back to where he was. Talking to him now, she knew for sure that that force was her love for him.

No more guessing games. No more doubt. Only true love.

The next morning when Kate woke up, she felt as if all her worries had lifted off her shoulders. She glanced at her laptop, which she had once again left in the bed beside her, and smiled.

"No more doubts," she said to herself. "If he can come see me soon, everything will be okay." But vacation time was over—it was back to reality, and that meant back to work.

Around mid-morning, her phone rang. It was Sara.

"Hi Sara, you are already missing me?" Kate answered cheerfully.

"Yes, honey, I'm missing you. But listen to you, you sound high-spirited this morning. Did something happen?"

"Um, nothing. I just replied to him, and we had a good talk. That's all." She knew Sara would know who she was talking about.

"You talked to him? Hmmm... what made you reply to him?"

"I don't know exactly what made me. But I feel a lot better now that I did."

"Hmmm... what about the money issue?"

"Well, he still has it, but he said he's working on it."

"He didn't ask you to send him that money again?"

"No, he didn't..."

"Hmmm..." Kate could tell Sara didn't seem convinced. "I hate to say this, but... he may be letting you off the hook for now so that he can ask again later, once you're blinded by his love or something."

"He is not like that at all. You just don't know him as much as I do."

"Okay, but I'm telling you this because I don't want you to get hurt or scammed. You just need to be super careful."

"I know." Even though Kate felt automatically defensive over Edward, she knew Sara was just looking out for her. "You didn't call me to just ask about my 'love' life, did you?"

"Oh, I almost forgot. Jane's birthday is on Saturday, so Mary and I want to put together a surprise party. Let's get together and make a plan. Are you free tonight?"

"Sure, I don't have any plans tonight. Where?"

"My house at 7:00 pm. I'll fix something quick for dinner. Mind you that it won't be like your food, miss iron chef."

Kate laughed. "I like your cooking, Sara. See you soon!"

"Bye!"

By the time Kate finished her work and arrived at Sara's house, Mary was already there, setting a table for three. "I brought your favorite wine, cabernet sauvignon, Sara," Kate said, holding up the bottle. Sara poked her head out of the kitchen and beamed.

"Oh great, thanks! Let's open it and toast!"

"Toast to what?" Mary looked puzzled.

"Toast to our friendship or to our loveless life! Hahaha…" Sara laughed hard at her own joke.

"Or to both!" Kate couldn't help laughing equally hard.

"But I thought you have a 'love' life, Kate?" Mary asked jokingly.

"Oh, Mary, gimme a break. He is not even here," Kate sighed. Kate had ended up telling her and Jane about Edward, too. Just like Sara, they'd been supportive, comforting her and assuring her it was best to be cautious. And, just like Sara, they'd been adamant that she not send any money for any reason.

Kate was grateful to have such good friends. She'd missed them, and it felt like they were coming back together after letting life drag them apart. Someday, she would have to thank Edward for that too.

****

Edward sat at his computer, contemplating whether he should mention money to Kate again or just tell Aidan that the one in America didn't work out and that he would move on to the next name. He had to buy some time until Henrik delivered the letter to Kate. Edward wasn't sure how long it would take Henrik to find her once he arrived at Stanford. Even if she was listed in the phone book, there were probably many "Kate Flemings," and it would take time to find the right one. If she wasn't listed in the phone book, it would probably take much longer to find her–internet searches could only do so much.

Edward wished he could've told Henrik more about her. In hindsight, he doubted his caution and wondered whether he could've carefully gotten more useful information from Kate without drawing Aidan's notice. But it was too late now. If Henrik's task turned out to be impossible, then at least Henrik would be safe in America.

Edward's thoughts were interrupted when the office door flew open. Aidan burst into the room and began his usual rounds around the room. Edward's heart sank. If Aidan was in the office, it meant he was expecting payments–which meant that he would definitely ask Edward about Kate. Edward sighed and waited for Aidan to reach him, and sure enough, he strode up to the desk just a few minutes later.

"It's been more than three months since you started talking with that American, Edward. You said she needed time to warm up, and I generously let you focus on her. But I don't see a single *sen* for all that trouble. What the fuck is taking you so long?"

Edward thought quickly. It was reckless to lie, but he was scared to know what Aidan would do if he wasn't convinced the payoff was worth all the time Edward was spending on Kate. "I think she's getting the money together. She just needs a little more of a push." Hastily, he added, "Don't worry, I've been looking at the list. I already have some names picked out for when I'm done with this one. Things just got a little hectic with Henrik leaving and all."

Aidan slammed his hand on the desk, and Edward flinched. But then Aidan said, "Fine. But if you don't get any money by the end of the month, you move on, and you put in double–no, triple the work for the next girls. Got that?"

"Got it, thanks." Edward was relieved; he couldn't rely on Aidan's fondness for Henrik much longer, but today it worked. He waited until Aidan walked away, then slumped in his chair.

He would have to find some abandoned Facebook accounts to start messaging or something. Edward really didn't want to start talking to someone new. He only wanted to chat with Kate. He sincerely hoped that Henrik would find Kate and hand the letter to her soon.

TEN

Henrik had a big mission: to find a woman named Kate Fleming. But how was he supposed to do that? He had no idea.

He'd landed at the San Francisco airport yesterday and taken a bus to Palo Alto, where Stanford University was located. He'd initially wanted to travel around the United States before school began, so he hadn't made any hotel reservations anywhere. But his father's frantic whisper at the airport had changed all of his plans. Fortunately, he'd found a hotel downtown with a room available. Exhausted, he went straight to bed.

As soon as he woke up the next morning, he booted up his laptop. While it was starting up, he took a quick shower. After he got dressed, he called for room service and ordered some breakfast. He googled Kate Fleming as he ate, but unsurprisingly, there were too many results to be useful.

"I guess her name is a common name in America. I wish Dad gave me a bit more information about her, like where she works or something," sighed Henrik.

After he finished eating his breakfast, he went out to get some fresh air. He took a leisurely walk down University

Avenue, window shopping and people-watching. He went into some shops and browsed around with no plans to buy anything. When he came out of the last store, which was a bookstore, he realized that he had spent a few hours there–it was already lunchtime.

He found a nice little café with tables and chairs outside on the sidewalk, which reminded him of the ones in Europe. After he sat down, a waiter–a young man who didn't look much older than Henrik–brought him a menu and asked if he wanted a drink. Henrik ordered a glass of lemonade. When the waiter returned with his lemonade, Henrik was ready to order. "I think I'll have a roast beef sandwich."

"A good choice," said the waiter, but instead of taking the order to the kitchen right away, he said, "Are you the new kid on the block?"

"The new kid on the block?" Henrik repeated. His confusion must've shown on his face.

"Yeah, that means you just got here."

"Oh, I see. Yes, I just arrived in Palo Alto yesterday."

"Where are you from?"

"Malaysia."

"Malaysia, huh?"

"Are you traveling?"

That was tough to answer. Henrik still hoped he would have time to vacation, but he didn't want to let his father down, either. He decided to be optimistic. "Yes, for now. I'll start my junior year at Stanford in September."

"No kidding! Me too. What's your name? I'm Mike." He held out his right hand. Timidly, Henrik shook it.

"My name is Henrik. Nice to meet you."

"Yeah, good to see you. Be right back."

After about ten minutes, Mike returned with the

sandwich. "Here's your roast beef sandwich. Listen, I'm getting off in a few hours. Do you wanna hang out?"

"You mean to spend time together?"

"Yeah, do you wanna?"

"Um… sure."

"Good, where are you staying?"

"Um… at the Garden Hotel."

"Okay, I'll meet you in the lobby at six." With that, Mike left Henrik's table to welcome the new customers who'd just walked in.

Henrik observed him for a little while, and it quickly became clear that Mike was very friendly with everyone. He wondered if all Americans were like him. Maybe Mike could help him find Kate Fleming, as Henrik still had no idea how to find her. That would save him a lot of trouble.

He had several hours to kill, so Henrik decided to go visit the university. According to Google maps, there was a museum on campus about two miles from the café. He decided to walk so that he could take some photos on the way, and as he got closer to the campus, he noticed more and more young people doing the same. Once he got there, he found he liked what he saw: red tile roofs, archways, thick walls, and an enclosed courtyard. Trees were abundant and provided nice shade. He soon found the museum, where he spent a few hours. It was a shame Edward couldn't have joined him; Henrik knew his dad would've loved it.

Henrik stayed on campus until about 5:30 pm, then decided to head back. When he got to the hotel lobby, Mike was already there, waiting. As soon as he spotted Henrik, he smiled at him.

"Hey, over here."

"Sorry to keep you waiting."

"Not really, I just got here myself. Where did you go after lunch?"

"I walked around the campus and visited the museum. I really like the campus. I'm so glad that I'm here," Henrik knew he was beaming, but he wasn't embarrassed. If he liked something, he was always proud to say it.

"That's good. Yeah, Stanford is pretty nice. Now what do you wanna do?"

"Um… I don't know. I don't know the area, so you can decide."

"Are you hungry?"

"Yeah, I am. Come to think of it, I haven't had anything since lunch."

"Let's go eat something. I know a good Japanese restaurant. You like Japanese food, right?"

"Yes, I love it."

They fell into a lively conversation as they started walking toward the restaurant. To Henrik, it was like they'd been friends for years.

****

The end of June was fast approaching. The day was long, and early summer vibes were in the air. The evergreen tree had full blossoms and its green leaves shone in the sunlight. Kate's garden was also in full bloom. She loved trees and flowers; thus, she had planted many of them over the years.

Kate had a full house with her children and their significant others. Dominique and Tren had their graduation ceremony a week ago and came to Palo Alto right after. It was a wonderful ceremony. Kate, Miki, and William had all gone to witness Dominique's proud moment. William brought Laura to the graduation, and Miki brought her new friend, James. Kate had been the only one by herself. She'd wished

Edward were there, too, but she resolved to tell him all about it as soon as she had time.

With four young people engaged in such a lively conversation, there wasn't a single quiet moment. Kate quietly observed them as she drank her tea. Eventually, William turned to her.

"... So, Mom, Aunt Jane's birthday is this Saturday, right?"

Kate's friends were like aunts to both William and Dominique, and they always referred to them as such.

"Yes, but it is a surprise party, so keep it hush hush, okay?"

"Got it. And where will it be?"

"At Aunt Sara's house at noon."

"Mike texted me this morning saying that he is bringing someone with him, though not a girl."

"A boy?"

"Yeah, he said he just met him at the café where he works."

That was interesting, though not necessarily unusual. Jane's son had always been incredibly outgoing, and even as a little kid, he made friends wherever he went.

Kate looked at the clock on the wall. It was almost 8:00 pm. Edward would be around soon, and she wanted to tell him about the graduation. Even though she knew she could send him messages at any time, she liked seeing his immediate responses. By now, it was second nature to align her schedule with his. She told everyone that she had to do some work, then got up and left the kids to their conversation. When she walked into her office, she made sure to close the door all the way. She then sat down at her desk and opened her laptop.

She and Edward had easily fallen back into their routine. Often, they only spent time talking about what they did on a given day, and that was enough. She felt content even when she didn't have much to say, because she knew that he was thinking about her. Privately, she believed they had an invisible connection. Fate, destiny... whatever it was, it made her happy.

She knew it was still possible that he was a scammer. She continued to ask Edward when he could come see her, and even offered to go to him, but he remained as elusive as ever. But Kate no longer cared. She wouldn't send him money, but she wouldn't cut him out, either. She loved him, and she would keep loving him until the day he ended things between them.

****

Mike and Henrik had just finished eating and were having green tea ice cream for dessert. Henrik found Mike extremely easy to talk to; they'd already shared all kinds of stories, and Mike didn't mind when Henrik asked him questions about American culture.

"So, what's your major, Henrik? I totally forgot to ask."

"Engineering. How about you?"

"Science. I wanna be a marine biologist."

"That's great!"

"Yeah, I love the ocean. Why do you want to be an engineer?"

Henrik shrugged. "My dad is an engineer, so I just thought I'd go into the same field."

"Hmmm... where is he?"

"He's in Malaysia."

Unbidden, Henrik recalled what his dad told him at the airport. He was certain that his dad was anxiously waiting to hear from him about the letter and Kate Fleming, but he had nothing to report. He'd sent his dad an email when he landed in America, but he hadn't had much to say. He wanted to ask for more information about Kate Fleming, but he refrained from doing so, as he remembered his dad's behavior at the airport. It was obvious his dad wanted to keep this Kate person a secret.

Mike tilted his head, frowning, and Henrik realized he'd gone quiet.

"Henrik, are you okay? You got awfully quiet. Did I ask something wrong?"

"Oh no, sorry about that. I was just thinking about my dad."

"Okay then..." Mike was quiet for a moment. When he spoke again, his cheer sounded a little forced, like he was trying to distract Henrik. "Oh yeah, this Saturday is my mom's birthday. Her friends are planning a surprise party for her. You wanna come? You should come. My other friends will be there too."

"Um... thanks, but I don't know. I don't want to impose..."

"Nonsense. You'd be my guest."

"Okay, then. I'll come. What should I bring?"

"Don't worry, you don't have to bring anything... but maybe some flowers, if you want? My mom loves flowers."

"Yeah, that's a good idea! I'll bring some flowers. Thanks, Mike."

"No problem." Mike polished off the rest of his ice cream, then looked at him again. "It's kind of personal, so I hope you don't mind my asking this, but how come you're already here, like three months before school starts?"

"Well, I wanted to visit a lot of cities in America before school began. But it looks like I might need to stay in Palo Alto for some time. I don't know for how long, though...I probably have to find an apartment."

"Why do you have to stay in Palo Alto?"

Henrik hesitated. He wanted to tell Mike everything, but

he didn't want to betray his dad's trust. He settled for being vague.

"…Um, I need to find someone who may or may not be living here…"

"Hmmm… who? Your girlfriend?"

"No, nothing like that."

"Who are you looking for then?"

"Um, I can't tell you that, sorry. It's a thing with my dad."

Fortunately, Mike didn't seem to mind. He looked thoughtful, then snapped his fingers. "You know what? You should come stay in my house until you find that person. I'll help you find them."

"Oh no, I can't do that. You've been very kind, but that's too much."

"Why not? We've got an extra room, and there's still so much time before the dorms are open, you can't spend all that money on a hotel. But if you want, it can just be until you find the person." Mike looked determined.

"But…"

"No buts! Let's go back to the hotel to get your things." Mike had already picked up the tab and was on his way to the cashier before Henrik could hurry after him. They walked back to the hotel, still engaged in a lively conversation.

When they arrived at the lobby, Mike said, "I'll wait for you here. Take your time, okay?"

"Thanks, it won't take long." Henrik ran up to his room and packed quickly. Luckily, he hadn't had much time to get settled in his hotel room, so it only took about fifteen minutes to pack, head back down, and check out. Mike was sitting on the couch, reading a newspaper. When he saw Henrik, he put the paper on the table and got up.

"All set?"

"Yes. Are you sure it's okay for me to stay in your house? Did you ask your mum?"

"I texted her just now, and she said it's fine."

"That's good."

Mike picked up one of Henrik's suitcases and headed toward the exit. Henrik hurried to follow him.

Mike's house was not far from the hotel. After about ten minutes, Mike pulled his car into the driveway. Both boys climbed out of the car and got Henrik's suitcases, then wheeled them to the front door. Mike told Henrik to wait and walked into the house. After a few minutes, he came back and motioned for Henrik to come in. Dragging his suitcases, Henrik stepped inside the house and proceeded to the living room where Kate and Jane were sitting.

****

When Kate saw Henrik, her heart jumped a little, though she couldn't understand why. He reminded her of someone, though she couldn't quite tell whom.

"Henrik, this is my mom, Jane, and this is her best friend, Kate."

For some reason, an odd expression passed over Henrik's face. Before Kate could ask about it, he recovered and turned to Jane.

"How do you do, Mrs. Wilcox. Thank you very much for letting me stay in your house. I'm very grateful." Then, Henrik turned to Kate and smiled slightly, but did not say anything.

"You're so welcome. You must be tired, so we can talk more tomorrow. I've already made your bed."

"Thanks again."

As Mike and Henrik started to go upstairs, Henrik suddenly turned to Kate. "It's nice to meet you, Mrs...?"

Kate opened her mouth, then paused. "...Smith. Kate Smith. And you don't need the 'Mrs.'."

"Okay, Ms. Smith. Nice meeting you, too," Henrik said. Kate thought he looked a little disappointed, but she had no idea why.

"Are you here on vacation?"

"Yes, for now. But I'll start at Stanford in September."

"Oh, how wonderful!"

"Where are you from?"

"I'm from Malaysia."

"Okay, we're gonna crash now, if you don't mind," Mike interrupted.

"Oh, I'm sorry. Go ahead. Didn't mean to stop you here," Kate said, a little embarrassed.

When the two boys disappeared upstairs, Jane asked, "Why did you say your name was Kate Smith?"

"Oh, I've been thinking about changing my name back to my maiden name for a while. It's been over ten years since I got divorced, and I'm still going by 'Fleming.' It's time to go back to Smith. I want to close that part of my life and move on. Don't you agree?"

"Yeah, I suppose it makes more sense."

"I wanted to say it to someone I don't know and see how it sounds. It's been so long, but I think it feels good."

It was getting late. Kate got up to leave, but her thoughts were still on Mike and his friend. At the front door, she said suddenly, "You know, Jane, I don't know what it is, but I feel like I've seen that boy somewhere."

"You mean Henrik? Where?'

"No idea. But something about him is familiar… do you know his last name?"

"Yea, Mike said something like… Edwardsson."

"Oh, Edwardsson… Hmm… Okay, never mind. I'll see you Saturday. Thanks for the wine."

"You're welcome. Yeah, see you Saturday. Good night."

"Good night."

All the way home, Kate kept thinking about Henrik, wondering why he seemed so familiar. As soon as she arrived at her house, she checked her phone and saw a message from Edward. Right on time.

They talked for a while, as usual. Edward mentioned something extraordinary may happen to them soon, though he did not elaborate on that, and Kate did not ask for details. Edward liked to make grand promises, but until he proved it and came to see her, Kate knew better than to believe him. For her part, she simply told Edward that her friend's son had made a new friend: a nice boy. She didn't mention his name.

ELEVEN

On Saturday morning, Kate, Mary, and Sara went over the last-minute details of Jane's surprise birthday party. They had invited over fifty people to the party. Jane was turning forty-five, and though it wasn't really a notable milestone, they still wanted to make it a big deal for her. The party would start in one hour. Jane was on her way to Kate's house because Kate needed to keep her distracted until she received a call from Sara.

Totally unsuspecting, Jane arrived at Kate's house a few minutes past eleven. It was Kate's job to keep her occupied for half an hour, just until the party was ready. Kate watched Jane get out of the car and walk toward the front door, but she waited until Jane rang the bell to go open the door. They hugged each other. When Jane did not see anyone else in the house, she asked, "Where are Sara and Mary? I thought the four of us were meeting this morning."

"Oh, Sara said she'd be tied up until three, and Mary said her mother had a small emergency, but she'll be back this evening. Then, we can all go out to celebrate your birthday!" Kate tried to look casual, and luckily, Jane bought it.

"Good. Can't believe I'm turning forty-five," Jane said, shaking her head.

"I know. I'll be forty-five soon, too… Do you want some coffee?"

"Yeah, I'll have some, if you already have a pot made."

"No, the drip is the best. I'll make it real quick."

Kate had to keep Jane occupied until Sara called, and she'd invited her over under the pretense of asking for advice. But now that they were together, she couldn't come up with anything to ask. She poured some water in the kettle and put it on the stove then went to grind some coffee beans. Jane chatted away, but Kate only responded with "uh-huh," "yeah," and so on. *Oh, c'mon, Sara. Call now. I'm not good at making small talk and I don't know how much longer I can hold on here.* She set up the drip coffee maker and gradually poured the hot water. In a couple of minutes, the smoky and nutty aroma of coffee wafted through the kitchen.

"Mmm, the aroma of good coffee…." Jane closed her eyes and inhaled.

"Here, the best drip coffee you've ever tasted, haha." Kate put a cup of coffee in front of Jane, then continued, "How are Steve and Mike?"

Jane held the cup with both hands and sipped her coffee. "Wow, this is so good. Oh, Steve and Mike? They're just fine."

"Good… where would you like to go this evening? Your favorite Italian restaurant downtown?"

"Yeah, that would be great. I just love that restaurant. Don't you?"

"Yeah, it's a nice place. I really love their desserts. They have all kinds, and their portions are just right," Kate said, a little awkwardly. Jane was a bit of a gourmet, and Kate was hoping she would talk about the restaurant more. But Jane was also the sort of person who got to the point straight away.

"So, you said you needed to talk about something?"

"Um… you know… I need…"

Kate's phone rang as she tried to think of something. *Phew! Saved by the ringtone!* She answered quickly. "Hi, Sara, what's up? Jane is here. I was just telling her why you and Mary aren't here. Uh-huh… Uh-huh… oh my god! We'll be there right away!"

"What happened?" Jane asked as soon as Kate hung up.

"She said she needed us to get to her house right away, because she had found a big spider in her bedroom. You know how she gets around spiders."

"Oh! Ugh, I hate spiders so much. You know, at a time like this, I wish we had a man around. Don't you agree? Let's go. Maybe three of us can tackle it!"

Kate and Jane picked up their purses and ran to Kate's car. Quickly, they drove off, and got to Sara's house in no time. As Kate parked in the driveway, Sara came running out of the house. "Oh, I'm so happy that you two are here! I couldn't reach the kids. Come, hurry! It'll be a complete disaster if it moves to the other part of the house and I can never find it!"

The three women ran to the front door. Sara opened it, and they heard:

"Surprise!" Immediately, people started singing. "Happy birthday to you! Happy birthday to you! Happy birthday dear Jane! Happy birthday to you!" There were many smiles and a lot of clapping. Some people blew the party horns, while others threw a lot of confetti all over the place. Jane looked completely dumbfounded, but she was clearly touched.

"Guys…" she began, but she fell speechless.

"Happy birthday, Jane." Kate, Sara, and Mary said together. They each hugged Jane in turn. Jane was in tears, but tried to keep her composure.

"I had no idea you planned this. But thank you so much. You're the best!"

The four women walked in and spread out to mingle. Mike and his new friend, Henrik, quickly came up to Jane. Henrik handed her a bouquet of flowers. "Mrs. Wilcox, happy birthday! This bouquet is for you."

"Wow, they are so beautiful! I love flowers! Thank you, Henrik."

"You are very welcome. Actually, it was Mike's idea that I bring some flowers for you, because you love them."

"Mike's idea?! I didn't know he had a sensible side."

"Yeah, mom, I can be sensible. Do you love me more now?"

Everyone laughed and cheered. Kate, Mary, and Sara sat down to chat while Jane made the rounds and thanked everyone for coming. After about half an hour, she returned.

"You guys really pulled this off! I was completely surprised!"

"Yeah, that's why it's called a surprise party," Sara said, looking somewhat proud.

"Yeah, but it's a good thing Sara called me earlier than planned, or else I might've spilled the beans. My poker face is terrible, you know?" Kate smiled at Jane.

"The four of us are still going out tonight to celebrate, right?" Mary chimed in.

"Yes, ma'am," Sara chuckled. Kate was happy, surrounded by her good friends. Privately, she wished Edward were there, as she often did when she had something nice she wanted to share with him.

That night, the four of them went to Jane's favorite restaurant, as promised. Kate had a wonderful time with her friends, talking and laughing like they were young college students again. But whenever there was a lull in the conversation, she couldn't help but notice that there were many couples in the restaurant. Inevitably, she felt a pang of loneliness, and couldn't help but wonder when she and Edward would be together.

****

Two months had already passed since Henrik arrived in Palo Alto, and he still couldn't find Kate Fleming. He was getting stressed out, especially because September was rapidly approaching, and he didn't want to be caught up in his search when school started. He'd looked online in every way he could think of, but it was impossible to tell what was real information and what wasn't.

He'd thought about sending messages on Facebook, but he didn't like using it; besides, when he searched for "Kate Fleming," too many profiles popped up. Messaging every single one would take forever. He thought about placing an ad in the newspapers for a missing person, but he didn't think that was what his father wanted. He wanted to email Edward and ask for help, but father's emails had been sparse lately, so he was probably busy. Henrik also didn't want to disappoint him by admitting he hadn't found Kate Fleming yet.

He wanted to ask Mike for help, but every time he thought about it, he remembered his father's hurried whisper. It had to be tied to the reason Edward had sent him to Iceland before America, but Henrik couldn't even begin to guess what was going on with his father. It was hard to keep secrets from Mike, though. They got along tremendously, and Henrik cherished him like family. Mike's older brother, Steve, stopped by the house from time to time, and the three of them often hung out. Plus, Mrs. Wilcox and her friends were kind and always cared for Henrik. He felt grateful to all of them, but he particularly liked Kate. She was super nice and thoughtful. If only her name was Kate Fleming.

Finally, he decided to ask Mike for help as subtly as he could. He stuck his head into Mike's room and called his name.

"Hey, Henrik. What's up?"

"Um… are you busy right now?"

"No, not really. I'm just doing my pre-reading for biology."

"Oh, I can come back later."

"That's okay. Do you need something?"

"Well… remember when we first met at the café, I told you I was looking for someone?"

"Yeah, I remember. Did you find them yet?"

"No, I would have told you if I had."

Mike made an understanding noise. "So, you're still looking."

"Yeah, but I'm not getting any leads or anything. So I wanted to ask you where I could go to try and find someone."

"Hmmm… let me see… you already checked online? Maybe the phone book or something?" Henrik nodded, and Mike drummed his fingers on his desk, looking thoughtful. "I'm not a hundred percent sure, but maybe you can go to City Hall?"

"City Hall?"

"Yeah. You'll probably have to fill out some kind of application, though. How much do you know about this person?"

"Um… not a lot. But if I go there in person and explain, maybe they can help?"

"I doubt it, but you can try."

"Okay, I think I'll try to go there today."

"Do you want me to go with you? I wanted to get some fresh air anyway."

"Will you? That'd be great, I still don't know my way around. Thanks Mike!"

"No problem, dude. Let's hit the road."

It was late summer in Palo Alto, but the temperature hadn't broken eighty degrees. Unlike Malaysia, the humidity was low, and it was pleasantly cool in the shade. Henrik liked California weather. Many people wore T-shirts and shorts with flip-flops. Very casual, very Californian. Henrik would have to buy himself more T-shirts, too. When they arrived at City Hall, they went straight to the information desk, where the girl behind the counter directed them to the clerk's office. After about half an hour, Henrik's number was called.

His hopes were dashed immediately. Without a birth date or a social security number, there was nothing they could do for him. Plus, they said, only relatives could obtain personal information this way. Henrik tried to appeal to them by saying he'd come all the way from Malaysia and that it was very important to find the person he was looking for, but the clerk wouldn't budge. They half-heartedly recommended hiring a private investigator, but from their doubtful expression, Henrik assumed they were just trying to make him feel better. He was disappointed, but there was nothing he could do. He returned to where Mike was waiting and told him the bad news.

"Hmph, what a bummer!"

"Bummer?"

"Disappointment."

"Ah, yes. A big disappointment…"

They stood up and started toward the exit. Then, Henrik saw Kate walking toward them. Henrik smiled and called out, "Hi, Mrs. Smith."

"Oh, hi Henrik. Hi Mike. How are you? What are you guys doing here?"

"Um, I came to ask about someone I'm looking for, but they can't help," Henrik said.

"You're looking for someone?"

"Yes. I've already searched all over the Internet, but to no avail. This place was the last hope…"

"Oh, I'm so sorry. If there is anything I can help with, just let me know, okay?"

"Yes, thank you."

"What are you doing here, Kate?" Mike chimed in.

"Oh, it's just the personal stuff." Kate looked at her watch. "Well, I'd better go, because my appointment is in a minute. I'll see you soon, huh?"

They said goodbye and parted. Henrik kept looking back at Kate all the way until they exited the building.

TWELVE

Someone else felt frustrated these days aside from Henrik. Edward, too, was getting frustrated day by day. There was still no news from Henrik regarding Kate. And Kate, oblivious, continued to ask when they could meet in person. Not to mention Aidan, who was breathing down his neck for the money. Edward felt cornered with no way out.

> I'm really getting frustrated, Edward... how much longer do I have to wait? And why can't I come see you?

I know... Just a little bit longer, dear.

I promise I'll come see you soon. Please be patient, Kate...

> That's all you've been saying for weeks. Sometimes I wonder if you really want to meet me.

Oh, Kate, don't say that. I do want to see

you as soon as I can.

But I just can't leave the country right now. I wish I could tell you when, but it's just not up to me. I'm really sorry.

If it's not up to you, then up to whom? I don't understand.

I know, I'm sorry... but please believe me and trust me on this. That's all I ask of you right now. Let's talk about something else, huh?

Edward wanted to scream, "If you read the letter I sent you, you'll understand everything. You'll understand why I can't say anything right now." But he couldn't say that, of course. Especially not when Aidan was circling around him like a hawk around its prey. He asked Edward incessantly when he was getting money.

"*Hey Edward, where's the money, man?*"

"*Um... coming soon...*"

"*And how soon is 'soon,' huh? I don't have time for whatever shitty game you're playing.*"

"*We just need to be patient.*"

"*Patient?! I think I've been very patient. You're months overdue!*"

"*I know, Aidan. Sorry.*"

"*Sorry won't bring us money. Get your fucking money!*"

Edward's answer was always the same: soon. That was all he said these days, "soon" to Kate and "soon" to Aidan. He was helpless, caught between them as he waited–for Henrik to tell him he'd failed, for Kate to tell him she'd gotten the letter, even for Aidan to lose his temper once and for all. But to Edward's surprise, Aidan did not force him to start a new chat, like he'd threatened. Edward was grateful for that, as he didn't want to start one ever again.

Aidan had thrown many threats at him over the years. Once, Aidan said he would tell Edward's parents in Iceland what Edward had done. Edward couldn't bear that his mom would find out about the drunken mistakes of his youth. Another time, Aidan threatened to tell Henrik the truth of his birth. Edward and Aidan got into a big fight in the office, so men had to intervene to separate them before one of them got killed. It was refreshing, not having to face that sort of thing again, but it left Edward feeling somewhat paranoid.

Every day, Edward cleaned his house and threw things away. It seemed that this was the only thing he could do while he waited to hear from Henrik. Every time he threw away a trash bag filled with his belongings, he assured himself that he was getting closer to his "getaway." Twenty years of living meant they had accumulated a lot of stuff, even though there were only two of them, and Edward had held onto most of it as a way to remember happy moments when he felt trapped and desperate. Now he was throwing away everything–well, almost everything. He wanted to keep certain items of Henrik's to remind himself of Henrik's childhood.

As he filled up a new trash bag, he wondered when, or if, Henrik would ever find Kate. He couldn't lose hope until he heard back for sure, because hope was the only thing that kept him going. He'd been honest when he told Kate he believed in faith, but it was getting harder and harder to hold on.

I've got to do something... but what can I do?

****

School started in September, and Mike and Henrik were on campus most of the day for five days a week. After their last classes, they went to the library to do their homework–sometimes together, sometimes separate. There were so many assignments from all the courses they were taking, they hardly had any time to hang out during the week.

Henrik missed his friend, but he was enjoying college life in America. He had moved into the dorm on campus a few weeks ago; his roommate was a nice guy from Thailand. Since they came from the same region of the world, they got along very well. But they, too, hardly saw each other during the weekdays, as they were both busy with schoolwork. Weekends were a totally different story. Mike and Henrik often got together and hung out, going to the movies or exploring nature. Henrik particularly enjoyed the California weather, which was completely different from Malaysia. Low humidity, dry weather, the blue sky…

He missed his dad from time to time, and sent brief emails to let him know how he was doing. Edward always replied with general statements and never asked about the letter, which was a relief, as Henrik still had it in his suitcase. Since school started, it seemed almost impossible to spend any time finding Kate Fleming. He had given up the online search, and he didn't think that his dad wanted him to place an ad in the papers or at the bulletin board on campus. Edward had urged secrecy, after all, and Henrik was too nervous to ask his father if he was in some kind of trouble. Still, Henrik wished he had a bit more information about Kate. He was tempted to open and read the letter just for some extra clues, but he wanted to respect his father's privacy. Besides, if it was really that urgent, surely Edward would have said something by now.

Even though he was anxious about finding her, the days

passed without any success as he got swept away by his schoolwork.

****

Kate, meanwhile, was getting used to using her maiden name again. It was a lot of work getting everything legally settled, but the more she did, the happier she felt. She had not changed it for Edward's sake, but she did think that it would be nice if someday, she could meet him only as herself, without any ties to her past marriage. Of course, he would have to keep his promises for that to happen.

Every time she asked, he always gave her the same answer: very soon. She had long since stopped believing him, but she couldn't persuade her heart to forget him. She loved him dearly. Whenever they spoke, she felt she was worth his time and attention. It had been so long since she'd felt that way—not just as a divorced mother of two, but as a woman worthy of love. He inspired her. No matter how disappointed she was with Edward's evasiveness, she couldn't put that aside so easily.

Her life, just like her garden, was full of color now. Every day, morning and evening, she made time for Edward—talking to him if he was around, or reading the messages he'd left while she was busy or asleep. She kept up her morning routines and her French lessons, but now she talked to her children a few times a week. Dominique had moved to San Francisco with Tren to work for a non-profit organization as a research associate. Tren was a mechanical engineer. William had started his sophomore year at Irvine. Miki, who was taking a break from traveling, came to visit her almost every day, and they had lunch or dinner together depending on when she came by. Kate had also taken to inviting her friends for dinner at least once a week, and got invited to their houses in turn. Things were good.

And yet... something was missing. And of course, that something was Edward's presence.

Edward, how do you do this?

What do you mean, Kate?

How are you so okay with not
seeing me? You won't even let me
video chat with you.

Who said I'm okay? I'm not...
But I have faith in us. I've told you a
million times since the beginning that
your love keeps me moving forward.

You keep telling me that I
must have faith. But what is faith
anyway?

It's trusting your heart to be honest. The
mind wanders everywhere all the time,
but the heart stays in one spot,
unwavering.

Your heart is what tells you to trust me,
isn't it? So I can only hope that you'll
trust it.

And when we're finally together, I
promise it will have all been worth it.

And you still can't tell me
when you can get here...

No, I'm afraid not...

Kate sat quietly for a while. She knew bringing up the topic would only cause pain and disappointment, but sometimes, she couldn't help herself. She wanted so badly to trust him, especially after she'd given him so much of her time, and her heart, already. Giving up on him now would feel like none of it had been worth it.

Kate, are you still there?

Yeah. I was just thinking.

I asked you this before, but I'll
ask again. Why don't I come see you, if
you can't come here?

I'm sorry, Kate. I already told you that it
won't work.

But why?

Because I want to come see you first.

That's not even a reason!

Kate, please don't make me feel guilty. I
already feel terrible about this whole
situation.

I'm not sure you do.

Kate, please. That's a little insensitive.

Who's talking about being
insensitive? You are the insensitive
one!

I know that...

Some of her anger deflated at how easily he accepted her criticism. But it still didn't make her happy, and she didn't know what else to say.

Kate, are you still there?

Yeah, I'm still here.

What are you doing?

Thinking. What are you doing?

Thinking.

About?

About us...
Kate, I know you are very frustrated right now. I don't blame you one bit. But let me try and explain how I feel right now.
You have given me a safe haven to

be myself and not to be ashamed of all the parts that make who I am. You have given me security that makes me feel safe and centered. You have given me a shoulder to cry on when I'm sad and a hand to hold when I'm lost in the dark.

We've talked about so many things–I know it's hard for you, but for me, it feels like I've been by your side all this time. I believe there is nothing we can't face together. You make me believe I can do anything I set my mind to.

There is a song I really like. It's called "You raise me up." It brings me a lot of comfort. Maybe if you listen to it, you'll feel the same way.

But please know that I'm always thinking about you, and about us together in the future.

Kate could feel tears welling up in her eyes. His words were so beautiful; it took her a minute to compose herself.

Thank you, Edward.

I'm sorry that I nagged so much tonight.

You don't have to apologize. I'm not upset. Believe me, I'm just as frustrated as you are.

I just want you to know that I love
you with all my heart. And I always will.

You're the one for me, Kate.

I love you too...

I think I'm gonna go to sleep
now. Sweet dreams.

Sweet dreams, my dear. Talk to you
tomorrow. Lots of kisses.

As soon as Kate shut her Mac, she wrapped her arms around herself and cried. She let her tears run down her cheeks and drop onto her shirt. She sat like that for a long time.

If she was going to trust and believe him, she would have to commit. She had to make up her mind. Edward always had the most beautiful, heartfelt words for her–and maybe she was deluding herself, but she didn't think they were lies. But it was clear that he wouldn't, or couldn't, say anything beyond what he had already told her for months. Pushing him would do no good; it would only make them both miserable. And since she didn't want to cut him out of her life… the only choice left was to believe in him.

The day would arrive when time was right. Until then, she would just enjoy what they had.

Something nagged at her despite this resolution, though. Setting aside the matter of his visit to California, she had always found it strange that he refused to call her or chat with her over video. And he had never given her a good reason for why she couldn't come see him in London. Even if he wasn't scamming her, he had to be hiding something. But what?

Maybe he's a serial killer! That was a scary thought; one she'd had before, but only as a joke. But if that were the case, he would want to meet her sooner rather than later. In reality, everything suspicious pointed to some typical money scam–but he'd stopped asking her for money eventually. It was all so strange.

Maybe he was in some kind of trouble. It was possible that he had a gambling problem, or something like that. Maybe it was worse, and he was trapped somewhere against his will. If that were the case, he wouldn't be able to say anything suspicious in their conversations. It was possible, then, that he wasn't even in London at all, but held captive somewhere else entirely.

She shook her head abruptly. "Yeah right, Kate. You watch too many movies," she told herself.

Getting up, she checked her phone and found a message from Sara asking to meet up for lunch tomorrow. Kate replied with an okay emoji. Sara had been worried about Kate's well-being for some time, ever since Kate had become content with her stagnant online relationship. To Sara, Kate and Edward were "going nowhere," and that kind of relationship was unhealthy.

Initially, she'd cautiously supported Kate's relationship. But as Edward continuously failed to keep his promises, she often told Kate to move on and find someone local. She even suggested that Kate sign up for an actual dating site, instead of wasting her time on a "Facebook weirdo." Sara herself had recently met someone on Match.com; thus, she strongly recommended that Kate do the same. She even offered to make her a profile.

Oh, don't tell me she made me one and wants to look at guys' profiles with me. Kate didn't want that at all.

The next morning, Kate pondered her wardrobe. Sara wanted to meet at noon at an Italian restaurant they liked–not too expensive, but fancier than a quick bite on their lunch breaks. That was strange, but she supposed Sara just wanted a treat.

She decided to wear a simple, classy black dress with a white sash around it. It was her favorite. She put on light make-up, then examined herself in the mirror. Though she was already forty-three, she knew she could pass for as young as thirty-five. She made sure that everything was in place in the house and closed the front door behind her.

THIRTEEN

When Kate arrived at the restaurant a couple of minutes to noon, Sara was not there yet. She told the hostess that she was meeting her friend Sara Forster, and she was taken to a table in the back. A couple of minutes after Kate sat down, she heard Sara calling her name.

"Kate! Kate!" As she turned to look, Kate noticed that Sara was walking toward her flanked by two men Kate had never seen before. When they arrived at the table, Sara asked, "Were you waiting for a long time?"

"Oh no, not at all. I was just seated."

"That's good." Sara beamed at her, then introduced the two men. "Kate, this is Eric, and this is his friend, Liam."

The two men extended their hands alternately to shake Kate's. Liam smiled at her. "Hi Kate, nice to meet you."

"Hi, nice to meet you, too." Kate threw a quick glance at Sara who shrugged her shoulders innocently. Kate quickly realized that Eric was the man Sara had met online, which meant that Liam was supposed to be *her* blind date. Sara and Eric wanted to be matchmakers this afternoon. *Ugh! No wonder she wanted to have lunch at this fancy restaurant. You owe me a full explanation after lunch, Sara Forster.* But she wasn't going to be rude, so she reluctantly settled in to learn more about the two men.

Eric Shaffer and Liam Hagerty both worked for a medium-sized tech company in San Francisco. Eric was a marketing manager, and Liam was a software programmer. They were serious basketball fans. When the waiter came to the table, Eric ordered a bottle of cabernet sauvignon, Sara's favorite red wine. Sara and Eric were busy talking to each other, and Kate felt a bit awkward. As if sensing her awkwardness, Liam broke the silence.

"Kate, what do you like? Do you eat anything?"

"Um… I stopped eating red meat about ten years ago, but I'm not a vegetarian. I love fish, so I could never give that up. How about you? Do you like everything?"

"Yeah, I can eat anything. But I'm trying to cut down on red meat–doctor's orders."

"But not entirely?"

"No, not entirely. It's just for my cholesterol. But I'm working on it." Liam laughed, clearly also feeling a little awkward. "I think I'll order fish today."

"Me too."

"Are you guys ready to order?" Liam turned to Sara and Eric.

"Yes, we're good." Eric called the waiter, who soon came to the table. Each of them placed their order. After the waiter left, Eric poured wine into four glasses and said, "Let's make a toast!"

"To what?"

"To love!" said Eric, smiling.

"To love," Sara, Kate, and Liam echoed.

They clinked their glasses and sipped the wine. It was good. Cabernet Sauvignon was Kate's favorite, too. Her ex had also liked this wine. It was probably the only thing he and Kate had in common. Kate wondered what kind of wine Edward liked; if he'd mentioned it, she couldn't remember.

Eric and Sara kept the conversation going as they ate. Liam spoke much less, as if he were an observer instead of a participant. Kate felt slightly awkward, because she suspected Liam was checking her out.

"Kate, what do you like to do when you're not working?" Liam finally asked.

"Um… I like movies, art, photography… outdoor sports too. Oh, and I love traveling. How about you?"

"I like pretty much the same things as you do. And basketball, like we were talking about earlier. Eric and I play with other buddies at least twice a week."

Eric turned as he heard his name, but he only smiled a little and quickly turned back to Sara. Kate looked at her plate awkwardly, but tried to keep her tone light. "Oh, I played basketball in high school. Not sure if I can still play, though."

"Oh, I'm sure you can. Do you want to play sometime?"

"Um… I don't know…"

"Oh, c'mon! Give it a try!"

"But it's been ages since I played, so…"

Liam was persistent. "Why don't we do this? Instead of deciding today, you can think about it. I'll give you a call next week to see if you're up for it. Is that okay?"

"Okay, that sounds good. Thanks for, um, being thoughtful." Kate looked at Sara and Eric who were still chatting away, absorbed in each other.

"You're welcome." When Kate didn't try to continue the conversation, Liam picked it up again. "I'm sure Eric must've told me, but what is it you do for work?"

"Um, I'm an IT translator for a Japanese company. Japanese to English."

"Really? Very interesting! Do you need a license for it?"

"No, you don't need anything like that." She wanted to say more about the IT stuff, but she hesitated for a moment, thinking of Liam's work. In the end, she continued, "To tell you the truth, I find IT stuff kind of boring. But at least I get to learn about new technology ahead of most people."

Fortunately, Liam didn't seem offended, he just laughed a little. "I have to disagree with you there. I really love my job."

"How long have you been working as a programmer?"

"Almost twenty years. A long time, huh?"

"Wow, yeah. You and Eric work together, right?"

"We work for the same company, but our jobs don't intersect that much. Sometimes we have meetings together, but that's it, really."

"Oh, I see. I didn't know that."

The rest of lunch progressed the same way. Occasionally, Eric looked over when he heard his name, but he never actually joined their conversation, and Sara, too, seemed to purposely want Kate and Liam to chat one-on-one. Fortunately for Kate, no one wanted dessert, and they left shortly after they'd finished eating. Kate thanked Eric for paying and politely shook his hand and Liam's; Sara shook Liam's, too, and hugged Eric goodbye. As soon as the men walked away, Kate turned to Sara with a serious look.

"Sara Forster, you owe me an explanation."

"I know, I know. I'm sorry I didn't warn you. Eric and I were talking and before we knew it, we were talking about introducing you and Liam. They're really good friends, you know. And since Liam's also divorced with two kids, we thought you guys were a perfect match."

Kate sighed. "Thanks for thinking of me, but I'm in a relationship now, in case you forgot."

"Oh, c'mon, Kate, you call that a relationship?! How long are you gonna keep that up?"

"What's that supposed to mean?" Sara gave her a look, and Kate frowned. "We will meet in person someday. I know we will."

"How do you know, huh? Your intuition? Some sixth sense? Kate, what you have with Edward is not real."

"I had the same thought in the beginning, but it's different now. You know how I feel about him."

Sara looked like she wanted to argue more, but she searched Kate's face, then seemed to deflate. But she didn't give up. "You can still go out with Liam and see if you like him. You need to go out more. Enjoy your life a little bit."

"But if I go out with him alone, he might get the wrong idea, so I don't want to do that." Even though Sara had set her up without permission, Kate knew it came from a good place, and she didn't like seeing Sara so worried over her. So, she offered a compromise. "The four of us can go out as a group. How's that?"

"I don't know, Kate. I think Liam really liked you."

"I doubt that, I wasn't a very good conversation partner. But if you're right, then we should definitely not go out alone."

"I'm worried about you, Kate. You are going nowhere with Edward. Your relationship with him isn't making any progress at all. Are you really content with that?"

No, she wasn't. But that was between her and Edward, and besides, she'd already decided to trust him. "Well, I'm not entirely happy about it, but I can be patient. I believe we'll meet soon."

Sara sighed. "Tell you what, why don't you think about Liam for a few days and see if you change your mind. Hm? Just try it, for me."

"I doubt I'll change my mind, but I'll think about it." Kate checked her phone. "I'd better get back to my work."

"Yea, me, too. I'll give you a call in a day or two."

They hugged each other and said goodbye. When Kate returned home, it was almost 3:00 pm. As she sat down at her laptop to resume her work, she felt a bit lethargic. Probably the wine. She went to the kitchen, and as she made some strong coffee, she thought about Edward and Liam.

The latter obviously had some advantages: first and foremost, he was local, and she could see him whenever she wanted. Like her, he was divorced and had two children around the same age. He was a year older than her. He had a good stable job that he was passionate about. Plus, Eric could vouch for him. On the other hand, she didn't have anything but words from Edward. Though he was also a parent, Edward was three years younger than her. As she thought about it, she realized she was always attracted to younger men. Ken had been a year younger than her; her ex-husband, two years younger. *What's up with me and younger men?*

She wondered if she should tell Edward about the date. She really didn't plan on seeing Liam again in private, but if Edward ever ended up in a similar situation, she would want him to tell her. "Who knows, maybe that'll make him act faster." With a chuckle, she felt better and finally began her work.

In the evening, she went to her mother's for dinner. Miki served salmon and fresh vegetables, and as they ate, she asked, "Anything new?"

"Yes, guess what happened today?"

"What?"

"Sara and her friend set up a blind date for me!"

"A blind date?" As Kate expected, Miki looked interested. "With who?"

Kate took her time finishing her bite of salmon before she answered. "A friend of Sara's new boyfriend."

"What does this man do?"

"He's a computer programmer in San Francisco. He's divorced with two children, but they live with their mother."

"Hmmm… he's local, huh? How old are the kids?"

"I think they're about the same ages as Dominique and William."

It was Miki's turn to fall silent, and Kate drank her iced tea as her mother slowly ate a piece of broccoli. Finally, Miki asked, "What did you think of him?"

Kate shrugged. "He seems nice. Considerate."

"You think you'll go on a date with him?"

"I don't think so… I mean, I don't know. Not right now."

"Why not?"

"*Why not?* I'm in a relationship with Edward!"

"You mean that online guy?" Miki looked like she couldn't believe Kate was still thinking about him. "He said he would come see you and never did, right?"

"… yes, that's right. But I believe in him."

"Kate dear, think carefully, okay? You have been divorced for over ten years and have not gone out with even one man since. Your love life has completely dried up. As far as I'm concerned, you needed a man yesterday. Here comes this nice, successful, local man. Why not give yourself a break? Go on a date with him and put some spice into your life."

"His name is Liam, by the way. But I don't know–what if I got into a relationship with him, and then Edward showed up? I would lose them both." Never mind that she wasn't sure she was even that attracted to Liam anyway.

"You wouldn't. You can just choose one over the other."

Kate scoffed. "Easy for you to say."

"Kate, be realistic." Miki patted her hand, then motioned toward the kitchen. "You want some dessert?"

Kate thought about it for a second, then shook her head. "No, I don't think so. Thanks for dinner, but I'm kind of tired, so I'm gonna go now."

"Okay, but I want you to think carefully about your situation with that online guy. It's not going anywhere, you know."

"I know, Mother, I know, but… anyway, good night. Talk to you tomorrow."

"Good night, dear. Drive carefully."

Miki walked her out, and Kate waved goodbye, then drove home. When she got inside, she sighed heavily, thinking about her mother's words.

Miki was right about one thing: It was time for Kate to get her own life back. She loved her kids, and she had worked hard to raise them, but she had given up so much of herself during that time. Though they hadn't needed her for some time, she had never really regained her sense of self. Not until Edward.

She had tried after the divorce, a little. After all, she truly wanted to meet someone with whom she could spend the rest of her life. She had been thinking about it seriously for the last couple of years. Since Sara, Jane, and Mary were also all single, they'd tried to meet new people at events, even a few parties. For them, boyfriends came and went. But Kate had never made any deep connections.

Then, eight months ago, she met Edward online. She still couldn't believe how deeply she cared for him. She loved him and wanted to build a future together with him. But when would that become a reality? Edward made promises and asked her for patience. But words were the only thing she had from him. Even now, their relationship felt like a dream–sweet and beautiful, but difficult to grasp. Liam, on the other hand, was real and tangible. He was nice, he lived close, and he had a stable job. He didn't make her uncomfortable, but she didn't feel the kind of connection she felt with Edward.

After she changed into her pajamas, she settled into her bed and messaged Edward.

> Hi Edward, how was your night?

A reply came instantly.

Hi Kate, my night was good, and how was your day?

> Super! Have you ever been on a blind date before?

No, I have not. Why?

> Well, I went on one today for the first time.

> Sara asked me to have lunch with her today. When I showed up at the restaurant, she was with two men. One of them was Sara's new boyfriend, and the other was my date.

Oh, I see. How did it go? Did you like him?

It went fine. He seemed like a
nice person.

Are you going to see him again?

I don't know... Maybe...

If you want to, you should.
But I'll be here thinking of you. Please
don't forget that.

You don't care if I date
another man...

Of course I do. But if I'm stuck here, I
can't stop you.

You could tell me not to go.

Yeah, but I choose not to, because I
respect your freedom.
　　After we meet, that's another story.
But I know you can't think of us as
together like I do until we meet. So if you
want to go on a date in the meantime,
that's okay.

Kate couldn't believe his reaction. First Sara and Miki, and
now Edward too? She had really expected him to protest. Was
it a Western way of thinking, to respect one's freedom to the
point of encouraging the one you loved to date another person?

Kate certainly behaved like a Westerner most of the time; however, her Japanese upbringing always surfaced when it came to relationships. When she was in a relationship with someone, she would not go on a date with another man. To her, it was a taboo. But then… was that old-fashioned? Were even the young Japanese people more flexible than her, these days? And if everyone was pushing her towards Liam anyway, was she just being stubborn? Maybe she should go, if Edward didn't see it as anything special.

Kate wavered back and forth, then finally made up her mind. Like Sara said, Kate needed to go out more. So, she could do lunch with Liam–as a friend or a colleague, not a date. She would make that clear. Just lunch; no more, no less.

FOURTEEN

Edward was in agony.

It wasn't that he had lied to Kate. He meant it when he said he respected her freedom, and that he wouldn't tell her not to go on a date if that's what she really wanted. But he had downplayed the shock and pain he'd felt upon reading her words. It had taken everything inside of him not to beg for her patience. He'd wanted nothing more than to write, *Please don't give up on me.*

He felt that he urgently needed to do something or he would lose Kate, which he couldn't bear to see happen. It had been almost four months since Henrik left home, and Edward had not heard any news from him about finding Kate. Edward had been naïve to think that Henrik could find her in a relatively short period of time. "Kate Fleming" was probably such a common name in America, even with the town narrowed down. What was he thinking?

Maybe he should talk to Aidan. Aidan might understand. It was a long shot, but it had already been twenty years since Edward's crime–the law would have forgiven him by now, even though Aidan clearly hadn't. It had never mattered to Aidan that Edward had been young, stupid, and unaware–all that had ever mattered to him was that his wife's child was Edward's, not his own. But Edward couldn't just sit back and lose Kate. And more importantly… he had paid for his mistake with his life for far too long. He had to stop letting his fear of Aidan control him, no matter how justified it was.

Aidan had not been around lately, but Edward resolved to talk to him as soon as he showed up. Only, he didn't. Not that day, nor the next. In fact, weeks passed with no sign of him, and Edward found himself wondering what had happened to him. When Edward needed him, he was not in the office, and when he didn't, he was breathing down Edward's neck. Edward asked around, but no one seemed to know Aidan's whereabouts.

Though he wondered where Aidan had gone, Edward certainly wasn't going to complain. If he were around, Aidan would certainly be asking about the money from Kate every chance he got. Edward couldn't even fault him for it anymore. Though the job itself was a sham, Edward couldn't deny that he was an employee who hadn't brought his boss a single *sen* in nearly nine months.

Things weren't supposed to happen this way. Edward determined a long ago that Kate would be the last woman he would ever scam. Initially, she was just the means to carry out his getaway plan. As soon as he received the money from her, he was going to take it and flee Aidan and Malaysia with Henrik. It had been a desperate, poorly thought-out plan, and looking back on it, Edward was sure he would have failed. Perhaps, then, it was fate that he had fallen in love with Kate. The realization that he wanted to spend his life with her had drastically altered all of his plans. And with Henrik getting accepted to Stanford as he had… Edward could only take that as a sign. Kate was worth changing his plans for. That was why he'd sent the letter with Henrik. That was why he was risking everything.

The letter was a gamble. If Kate didn't read the letter in time, or if she didn't believe its contents, Edward would have no choice but to remain at Aidan's mercy—or worse. Edward's life hung in the balance between his past, Aidan, and his future, Kate. Until Aidan returned, all Edward could do was wait and pray that Henrik would find Kate as soon as possible.

****

It was in the middle of October, and autumn was in the air in Palo Alto. The leaves were turning red, yellow, and orange throughout the city. Of course, there was no comparison with autumn on the East Coast, or in Japan where the leaves turned so vibrant everywhere, but it was still beautiful. The sky was vast and clear, and love was in the air. Couples were abundant in the cafés and in the parks, enjoying the cooling weather. Autumn was Kate's favorite season, but without a partner, it had turned dull. Every year since the divorce, autumn brought up feelings of sadness and nostalgia, and it had only gotten worse over the past few years.

After lunch, Kate decided to go out for coffee for a change. She had been cooped up in her home office all week. She decided to walk to a café only a few blocks from her house. Most people were still wearing T-shirts and shorts; Kate was dressed in the same way, but she had an oversized scarf around her neck just in case. She walked leisurely to the café, taking in the city view. As she approached, she noticed someone familiar sitting outside and reading the book. It was Henrik. She had not seen him since Jane's birthday. He seemed to have grown up a bit, or perhaps he was feeling more comfortable with California life.

"Hi, Henrik. Long time no see."

Henrik looked up. He seemed briefly surprised to see her, but then he smiled. "Oh, hi, Mrs. Smith—Kate. How are you?"

"I'm good. Thanks. What are you reading?"

"The textbook from one of my classes."

"Oh, then I'll leave you alone."

Kate turned and started to leave. But Henrik quickly responded, "No, it's okay. I wanted to take a break, anyway. Please sit down."

"Are you sure?"

"I'm positive. Please."

"Okay then." Kate sat down across from Henrik and continued, "How's Stanford?"

"Classes are hard, but I like it. I really love Palo Alto too."

"Yeah, me too. It's really diverse here because of Stanford. We get a lot of people from all over the world. I am one of them, and you too, right?"

"Right, but I thought you were from here. I mean, born here."

"I was born in Japan, but yes, I am an American with an American father and a Japanese mother."

"Really? Me, too. I'm mixed, I mean. My dad is from Iceland and my mom is Malaysian."

"Really? I didn't know that." A waitress approached as they talked–Kate ordered a latte, then turned back to Henrik. "Where are they? In Malaysia?"

Henrik's face fell. "Um, yes, my dad is there, but I'm not sure where my mom is. I think she's there, too. My dad never really spoke about her."

"You must miss them," Kate said gently. Henrik nodded, though he seemed distracted, like he was thinking about something else. The waitress's return seemed to startle him back to the present.

"Yeah, I miss my dad so much, but my mom... I don't have many memories of her, because she left when I was a baby..." Henrik trailed off. Kate felt a little awkward, unsure of what to say. She sipped her coffee and settled on, "I'm sorry to hear that."

"It's okay. It happened a long time ago. Maybe I will ask my dad about her when he comes here."

"Oh, is he coming here to visit?"

"No, not really. I mean, I don't know when. It all depends on the letter he handed me..."

"The letter?" Kate tilted her head, puzzled.

"Yeah, before I left Malaysia, he handed me a letter to deliver to someone. I have a feeling that when she reads it, he will be able to come here..."

"It's addressed to a woman?"

"Yeah."

"Hmmm..." Kate sipped her coffee again, thinking. "She must be an important person to him. But why the letter? Why can't he just come see her normally?"

"I don't know. He didn't tell me anything about her. He just asked me to find her and give her the letter."

"Hmmm... it's old-fashioned, but it's kind of romantic." She smiled at Henrik, who still seemed a little lost in thought. "What's her name?"

Henrik looked up at her, surprised. "Um, her name is K–" Abruptly, he cut himself off. "I mean, sorry, I can't tell you. It's kind of a weird situation, but... I'm not really supposed to tell anyone. I wasn't even supposed to talk about the letter, haha. Please forget about it, okay?"

"Ahh, of course. Sorry for asking so many questions." Still, she couldn't help commenting, "I'm guessing you haven't found her yet."

"No, I tried very hard, but I haven't been able to… I've been searching since I got here, but I haven't even found any clues about her."

"Can't you ask your dad? Call him."

"No, I can't. My dad said it's not allowed."

Kate frowned, setting her coffee cup down. "What do you mean 'not allowed'? You can't even call your dad?"

"We email each other, but I'm not supposed to talk about her at all."

"Why not? I don't get it."

Henrik shrugged, looking uncomfortable. Kate realized she was asking too many questions again; she felt a little embarrassed, getting so invested in the mystery. She checked her watch.

"Sorry, I've gotta get back to work. Good luck with finding her. Don't forget you're always welcome, okay? Come over if you need anything."

It worked; Henrik looked more relaxed. "Thanks, I'd like that. Nice talking with you, too, Kate. Bye."

****

A few hours later, Kate was relaxing on the terrace with a cup of tea after work. Autumn had arrived here, too. Her garden was full of fall colors. Around fifteen years ago, she'd brought a couple of Japanese maple trees back from Japan, and they'd grown tall and supple. Their striking red leaves were beautiful against the blue sky. There were many autumn flowers in the garden, too. Begonia, marigold, petunia, and many different types of roses. As she strolled around her garden, her thoughts went back to that mysterious letter. She was so intrigued by it, especially the mystery surrounding Henrik's father. Her phone rang while she was lost in thought. It was Sara, and Kate knew immediately why she had called. She sighed, but answered obediently.

"Hello, Sara."

"Hello, Kate. What are you doing?"

"Just walking around the garden, it's a nice evening."

"Nice." As Kate expected, Sara got straight to the point. "So, have you made up your mind about Liam?"

"Um… he seems like a good person."

"He is. Eric said Liam is really popular around the office, since he's so considerate."

"Yeah, I noticed that."

"So you want to see him again?"

"Oh, I don't know…" Kate sighed. She'd debated this very thing ever since her conversation with Edward, and wasn't entirely satisfied with the conclusion she'd come to. Still, she admitted, "I think I can have lunch with him, but not dinner or drinks."

"Okay, that's a start. I'll let Eric know and give him your cell number. Is that okay with you?"

"That's fine. How are you and Eric doing?"

"Oh, we are doing just fine. We've had a few dates so far, and on the last one, we finally kissed."

"That's nice. I'm glad." And she was, truly. But talking about Sara's romance just reminded her of Edward's failure to appear, so she changed the subject.

"Oh yeah, I ran into Henrik this afternoon."

"Oh, that kid from Cambodia? How's he doing?"

"From Malaysia, not Cambodia. He seems to be doing quite well. He said he really likes Palo Alto."

"That's good…Well I've gotta go. Expect that you will be hearing from Liam soon, okay?"

"Okay. No hurry."

"Yes, hurry!" With a laugh, Sara hung up. Kate shook her head and went inside to make dinner.

Sara had always told Kate that when an opportunity knocked, you had to grab it, because you didn't know when you would get a second chance. Kate couldn't argue about that. She had that opportunity right now. She should take it. Sara had also often told Kate that they weren't getting younger, which was also true. Since Jane's party, Kate had truly begun to feel her age; in just five years, she would be fifty. Her opportunities for romance were rapidly dwindling. Liam was, logically, her best option.

But what about Edward? As she ate her salmon and drank her wine, that was, as usual, the foremost thought in Kate's head. Sara, of course, had long since written Edward off as a scammer, or at the very least, a flake and a liar. But Kate had chosen to trust her heart, which meant trusting Edward. It was hard enough to go back on that even a little bit, and she fully expected that lunch with Liam would only feel like a betrayal. But at least if she went, she could appease Sara, and put the possibility of Liam out of her mind for good.

FIFTEEN

It took Aidan four weeks to come back to the office. Edward hated to admit it, but he had started to worry. It was pointless, though; shortly after his return, Edward learned from a coworker that Aidan had simply been in Japan on vacation. Edward wanted to be angry, and he was admittedly a little jealous–but mostly he was just relieved.

When he came into the office, Aidan seemed very relaxed and jovial. He'd brought back some cakes and cookies from Japan, which he began passing out. "Here, these are really good. They're not too sweet. Try some." If he noticed everyone exchanging nervous glances, he didn't show it; and, of course, no one dared to speak or refuse him and ruin his mood.

When he came to Edward's desk, there were only a few cakes and cookies left. "Here, Edward, try some. I know you don't like sweets, but these should be okay for you," he said cheerfully. Edward didn't want any, but he didn't want to wreck Aidan's good mood either, so he took one of the cookies and tried it. Surprisingly, Aidan was right–it was good.

It was tempting to put off talking to Aidan, but now was probably the best chance he was going to get. Aidan was in a good mood, happy and refreshed from a vacation. If there was ever a time he would grant Edward's request, it would be one like this. Edward popped the rest of the cookie in his mouth, then asked if Aidan had a few minutes.

"Yeah. What is it?"

"Can we go into your office and talk? I need a little privacy."

"Sure."

Edward followed Aidan to his office and shut the door behind them. Aidan sat at his desk and motioned for Edward to sit down in a chair at the other side of his desk. Edward did so.

"Well?"

Edward took a deep breath and did his best to meet Aidan's gaze, steady and serious. "Okay... Aidan, I want you to know that I appreciate everything you've done for me and Henrik for all these years, but don't you think I've paid off my debt to you by now? It's been twenty years. I've had enough of this kind of life. Now, I want to leave and start anew--"

"Leave?" Aidan interrupted. "Why? You don't like it here?"

He didn't sound angry. If anything, he seemed genuinely surprised. Edward's heart filled with hope. "To be honest with you, I never liked it. I stayed because I had Henrik. But now he is gone, and I am not sure if he will ever return after he finishes college. Nothing's keeping me here." Nothing except Aidan's threats. But Edward, of course, didn't dare say that.

Aidan tapped his fingers rapidly on his desk. "Where you going, man?"

"I don't know yet. I mean, I haven't decided. But I want to get out of here."

Aidan watched him for a while–long enough that Edward began to feel nervous again. Was Aidan playing with him?

Eventually, Aidan said, "I know. You fell for that American

woman in California, didn't you? What was her name? Katherine or Katrina or something? Am I right, am I right?" He grinned, as if they were two friends joking around, rather than a tormentor and his longtime victim. Edward swallowed hesitantly.

"No, that's not why. I'm just tired of doing this." At least he wasn't completely lying. He had planned to leave, even before Kate.

"Well, that's okay, you don't have to give me the reason." Aidan smiled, but it was cold. Edward's instincts warned him that it was too good to be true–and sure enough, Aidan's smile morphed into a glare. "But before you go, you pay me the money you owe me. You have been talking with that chick in America for nine months without getting a penny from her. Get the money from her, then you can leave."

This was tricky. If he admitted he didn't want to scam Kate, Aidan would know he'd lied, at least in part. But Kate definitely wasn't going to send him any money. What was he going to do?

"Ah… I don't think that's going to work, Aidan." He hesitated. He didn't really have much saved up, but he tried to offer, "Maybe… I could just pay you–"

"No. You've wasted all this time on that woman, so you get it from her. No one else."

"That's outrageous!"

Aidan shook his head. "You think I forgot the other times you were in here? You keep saying you want to leave, but you never do. If you really want to leave, prove it. Get the money from that girl you don't care about, and then you're free to go."

Edward looked back at Aidan with an equal glare, who whistled nonchalantly. Edward felt anger toward him, but didn't say anything. After a little silence, Edward got up and left his office. He felt Aidan's eyes on him all the way out.

When he returned to his desk, Edward felt his anger was surging, so he decided to step out of the office to cool off. It was raining hard outside. In fact, it had been raining for ten straight days. He stood under the awning and lit a cigarette, then exhaled slowly. He couldn't ask Kate to send him money again. She would definitely think that he was a scammer. She might stop talking to him once and for all, especially now that she had that blind date guy in her life. Edward let out a deep sigh, feeling ever so helpless.

He considered lighting a second cigarette, but decided against it. Kate would be online soon, and he didn't want to be late. He headed back inside and sat down, then sent his usual greeting. Simply typing it out made him feel better; some days, he thought these conversations were the only thing keeping him alive.

Hi Kate, how are you? How was your
day? Hope it was fine.

What did you do today?

Did you get your work done?

Did you eat your dinner already? Did you
save some for me?

Edward asked one question after another, channeling his frustration. A reply came almost instantly.

Hi Edward, I'm good. Are you
okay?

Sorry. I was really frustrated, but I'm
okay now.

> That's good. Why were you so
> frustrated? Your work?

Yeah, you could say that.

But it's more that I'm just so fed up with
my life here. I wish I could get out.

Belatedly, it occurred to Edward that Aidan could easily read this conversation—and likely would, after their earlier discussion. But he was still too angry to care much. Aidan would probably brush him off anyway, since he clearly didn't take Edward seriously.

> That doesn't sound good. You
> wanna talk about it?

Let's just say that my boss can be very
unreasonable.

> Your boss? I thought you were
> the boss.

Oh. Oops. He had to be more careful.

I meant the boss from the investment
company I'm dealing with.

So, did you go on a date with that blind-date man?

> No, not yet...

But are you going to?

> I don't know yet...

Do you want to?

> I don't know... maybe... since I
> got approval from you :)

I didn't give you approval.

> But you didn't stop me either.
> You encouraged me to go on a date
> with him.

I definitely didn't.

I just said that I can't tell you what to do.
I don't want to control your life,
especially from a thousand miles away...

As I said before, I respect your freedom.

> But you could still say no,
> don't go on a date with anyone...

This was one of the ways they truly differed. Edward

struggled to understand why Kate wanted him to boss her around so much.

Yeah, maybe.

How do you picture your future with me, Kate?

You mean like where we'll live
and stuff?

Yeah, I suppose...

Well... I lived in Japan and now
I'm in the US, so I think I can live pretty
much anywhere in the world. I'm fairly
adaptable.

I will probably continue
working as a translator, and you will be
working for some tech company as an
engineer. And I imagine...

We have quiet evenings to
ourselves during the weeknights, but
on the weekends, we go out for dinner
and movies. Alone or with our friends.
Sometimes we'll go to parties
or other events. Sometimes the kids
will come over.

We can go on a trip every year
for a few weeks. Anywhere we want.
Maybe go to art museums together...
Picasso, remember? Haha.

Just this ordinary stuff with my
family and friends... that's what I want
to do with you.

That's what I want too, Kate. I love you.

We'll be happy together as soon as I get
out of here, I swear.

Yes...
I have one request, though.

I want to live in a country where there is
very little humidity. I've had enough of it.

I didn't know London was that
humid. But I went there in the fall and
winter, so how should I know, huh?

Ugh! He was really slipping up.

Yeah. London gets humid sometimes...
and it's really awful.

How about Canada? I think
Canada has low humidity.

169

Yeah, Canada sounds great! Montreal or
Quebec?

Either city is fine with me. I've
been to both cities and liked them.

Nice.

Do you have any plans
tonight?

Just chatting with you.

Good.

Kate, you can't imagine how much I
want to be with you.

Once we're together, I'll never let you go.

I'm glad. Don't. Stay with me,
always.

****

San Mateo had a lovely Japanese restaurant called Kazu. Kate
had never been, but it was a comfortable, familiar cuisine, and
the location was perfectly equal for both herself and Liam, who
was coming from San Francisco. The November air had
quickly gotten cold, so she'd worn a silk scarf and a jacket over
her casual dress; when she spotted Liam, he was similarly
bundled up, but he greeted her with a big smile.

"Hi Kate. Thanks for coming out today."

"Hi Liam. Thanks for inviting me to lunch. Sorry I'm a bit late."

"No worries. I already put my name on the waiting list. Shouldn't be too long."

Kate offered him a smile. Despite everything, Liam was quite nice. It wasn't his fault she was already in love with another man. "Hope you like Japanese food."

"I love it. Who doesn't?"

"Occasionally I encounter people who hate it."

"Really? They just don't know how to appreciate good food."

"Yeah, I agree with you on that."

After chatting for about ten minutes, the hostess called Liam's name. When they were seated, a waitress came to the table and asked for their drink orders.

"I'll take a Kirin. How about you, Kate?"

"I'll just have some green tea. Thanks."

They examined their menus in comfortable silence. By the time the waitress returned with Liam's beer, they were ready to order. Kate ordered a shrimp tempura lunch box, and Liam ordered a teriyaki beef and a shrimp tempura combination box. They exchanged small talk while they waited for their food to arrive. When the waitress brought their lunch and left, Liam turned to Kate, looking determined. "Kate, why did you accept my lunch proposal today?"

Oh, he's bringing this up already. "Um, why not? I just thought that I should go out more often and socialize with people," Kate answered casually.

"Then, it didn't have to be me. You would've gone with anyone?"

"Well, not just anyone. Someone nice and trustworthy. Since we already met once, and you seem to be a nice person, I thought it would be fun to hang out."

"Well, thanks for the compliment. I think you're nice, too."

"Really?" Kate was a little surprised. She knew she'd been awkward and uncomfortable last time they met. "Thanks."

Liam got straight to the point. "Is this something you want to do on an ongoing basis? Going out with me?"

Kate hesitated. She'd been asking herself that same question. She knew her heart was with Edward, and she didn't want to lead Liam on. At the same time, Liam really was nice, and if nothing else, she wanted to be friends with him for Sara's sake. If Sara and Eric got serious, Liam would surely become a member of their group, and she wanted to have a good relationship with him. Then again, she knew a lot of men didn't like being "just friends" with women they were interested in...

"Kate? What's on your mind?"

"Um, nothing. To answer your question, I don't know... I can have lunch occasionally."

"Only lunch?"

"Yeah..."

Liam frowned. He looked at her closely. "Are you seeing someone?"

"Um... not really, but..."

"You *are* seeing someone." Liam sat back. "Are you in a serious relationship with him?"

"Well, it's kind of a complicated situation, and I'm not sure if I can explain it well."

"Try me. I'm listening."

Kate hesitated a little longer, but she didn't want to lie. At the same time, she didn't want Liam to think she was an unfaithful person, going out with him on a date when she was dating someone else. "Um, well... I've been talking to this guy online for about nine months now, but that's the extent of it. So far, it hasn't gone anywhere."

"You've been talking with someone for nine months and haven't met him face to face?"

"That's right."

Kate felt uneasy. Liam continued, "Don't you want to see him in person?"

"Of course, but he doesn't know when he can come see me…"

"Hmmm… did he say why?"

"No, not really." That was one of the biggest sticking points for Kate, but she didn't want to think about it too much. It had taken her so long to decide to trust Edward, and she had had to accept a lot of things she wasn't happy about.

Liam, of course, didn't know about any of that. He asked bluntly, "Did he ask you to send him some money?"

Kate looked at him, shaken. "…Um, yes he did once a while ago, but he hasn't lately…"

Liam looked lost in thought, but soon he said, "Kate, I'm sorry to tell you this, but I think he is scamming you."

It wasn't anything she hadn't heard before. Still, she asked, "How can you be so certain?"

"I'm just being realistic. Talking that long with nothing to show for it, and asking for money? He's just playing around with your emotions."

"…In the beginning, I thought so, too. But the more I talk to him, the more I think he is real."

Liam shook his head. "That's the dangerous thing. The more you talk, the more you become vulnerable. That's what those scammers are aiming for. When your vulnerability reaches its peak, then you cave in and send money. They're pros at figuring out just what to say and how to act to make you fall in love. It is amazing that you lasted this long without sending him a penny, Kate. Most women succumbed to their predator after only a few months."

Kate remembered the article she'd found, one she'd gone back and reread plenty of times throughout her relationship with Edward. *Romance scammers will express strong emotions for you in a relatively short period of time... they often come from western countries but are working overseas...*

"How do you know so much about online romance scammers?"

"Because I was one." Kate stared at Liam, frozen in shock. He stared back–then broke into a smile and laughed. "I'm just kidding. Sorry, it was a stupid joke. I've just heard a lot about them, that's all. You see stories about them in the news all the time. They confess their love quickly and start talking about the future together. They promise to come see you, which of course will never happen. Then, once you've fallen for them, they ask for money–and as soon as you send it, they vanish."

"But he stopped asking me about money." That, Kate thought, was a solid point in Edward's favor. But Liam didn't look convinced.

"He's probably using a different strategy to get more money out of you. Since you weren't easy to scam, I bet he's gonna try and get you to send him a lot, to make it worth it."

Kate shifted uncomfortably. "I don't know. I don't want to think that way."

"I'm sure you don't. It sounds like you're already kind of controlled by him, at least emotionally. You've been talking to him for so long that now, you are in the world he created and you refuse to see what's really happening."

Liam's last words were a blow to Kate. He wasn't saying anything she hadn't heard before–she'd had those very same thoughts for herself plenty of times. But Liam didn't know her that well. He didn't know her past, like Sara and Miki, and he didn't know the whole story of her journey with Edward.

Realistically, that should have meant she could dismiss his words easily–she knew how bad the relationship looked on the outside, and she should've been prepared to argue and defend Edward. But in reality, she could feel Liam's doubts adding to her own misgivings. His voice added to the many others telling her she was making the wrong decision. She pushed it away.

Firmly, she said, "Let's talk about something else."

SIXTEEN

Kate had wanted to do something different for Thanksgiving, but the day arrived too quickly, and she ended up with a typical sit-down turkey dinner with her family. Miki brought her boyfriend James, and Dominique, Tren, William, and Laura came over too. Kate also invited Henrik, since Mike was going to his grandparents' house with his mother. She thought about inviting Liam, but she had not seen him since that lunch two weeks ago, and though they had parted on a relatively pleasant note, it still felt too soon to include him in the holidays. He had called her a couple of times and asked for another lunch date, which she kindly declined, but she did agree to get together again soon.

Sara had also called; she was going to Eric's parents' house for Thanksgiving. Kate was happy for her. Her thoughts were suddenly broken by Henrik's surprised voice.

"Wow, did you make all these by yourself, Kate?" Henrik exclaimed, looking amazed at all the foods spread out on the table.

"Yeah, with some help from the stores," Kate said; she winked at Henrik, who blushed.

"Let's dig in!" Kate called out. The other kids were

watching TV in the living room, but they all quickly made their way to the table.

With eight people, there was not a single moment of silence. Someone was always talking and the conversation flowed. Dominique and Tren announced that they were planning a trip to Southeast Asia after the holiday–for two weeks, they would tour Vietnam, Cambodia, Thailand, and Malaysia. Henrik was delighted to hear they were going to his home country, and he and Kate–who still had her travel sites bookmarked–promised to give them lots of good advice.

"Do you celebrate Thanksgiving in your country, Henrik?" asked Miki.

"Yes, but in May, not in November."

"In May, huh? Do you eat turkey?"

"No, we don't eat turkey. We eat different kinds of dishes prepared with rice, and we drink homemade rice wine."

"Homemade rice wine! Sounds good! Do you like it?"

"Yeah, I love it, especially my dad's."

"Is he in Malaysia with your mom?"

"He is, but I don't know about my mom. She left when I was a baby…"

"Oh, I'm so sorry to hear that… you must miss your father very much, Henrik. Too bad he couldn't visit you now," Miki said. She looked sympathetic.

"Yeah, I miss him very much… Hopefully he can come visit for Christmas. He's a Christian, so we celebrate big on Christmas."

"Okay, mother, stop third-degreeing Henrik," Kate cut in.

"I'm not third-degreeing him. Just talking to him." Kate could tell Henrik looked a little relieved, though.

"Anyone ready for some desserts? I've got pumpkin pie, pecan pie, and mochi ice cream."

"I'll have all three, Mom!" William shouted, which made everyone laugh.

Henrik got up and started to take the dirty dishes to the kitchen. Kate said quickly, "Stop that. You are a guest, and the guest doesn't deal with the dirty dishes. Dominique and William can do it."

"I don't mind, Kate. Clearing the table is the least I can do." At a glance from Kate, Dominique and William jumped up to help–Tren and Laura followed suit, and with everyone helping, the table was cleared quickly. Kate shooed them out of the kitchen, then turned to Henrik once they were gone.

"Thank you, Henrik, for your help."

"You're welcome. I'm used to it. It was always just me and my dad, so since he cooked most of the time, I washed the dishes, you know."

"Is your dad a good cook?" Kate asked, as she moved to load the dishwasher. Henrik rinsed off the dishes in the sink, then helpfully passed them to her.

"Yes, he is. He always cooks my favorite foods."

"Have you talked to him lately?"

"I sent him an email a couple of days ago."

"Good. He must miss you very much…"

"Yeah."

"Did you find the person you were looking for?"

Henrik looked surprised–probably because she had remembered. "Oh no, I haven't. I was really busy with school, so I kinda forgot about it."

"But isn't it very important to your father?"

"I think so, but I'm not sure, because he didn't tell me much either way. When school gets out in a few weeks, I'll spend more time looking for her."

"Let me know anytime if you need help, okay?"

"Yeah, thank you. You are always so nice."

"You're welcome." Kate wanted to ask more about the letter, but she didn't want to be nosy, especially with so many others around. She didn't know why she was so interested, anyway. After dessert and coffee, Henrik bade them farewell; he politely declined the offer to stay over, as the other kids were doing. Kate made sure he caught his Lyft back to campus safely, then headed back inside, pushing her curiosity about the letter out of her mind once more.

Two days later, Dominique and Tren left for their trip. Kate stood at the security gate and watched them move inch by inch in the line. After about half an hour, they finally cleared security, and they waved and called goodbye. Kate called back, though she wasn't sure if they heard her.

On her way to the exit, she spotted someone familiar. It was Liam, and he was with a young woman. Kate thought she was seeing something she was not supposed to see, so she started hurrying back to her car, ignoring him. But he saw her and called her name, which meant she couldn't ignore him.

"Hi Liam." Before she knew it, Liam and the young woman were standing in front of her. Liam said, "Kate, this is my daughter, Lily. She came up for Thanksgiving and now she's going back to Los Angeles. Lily, this is my friend, Kate."

"Hi Kate."

"Hi Lily." Kate felt a bit awkward and couldn't come up with anything else to say. Fortunately, Liam broke the silence.

"Lily, I think it's time for you to go."

"Yeah, Dad. I'll see you in a month! I love you."

"Yeah, see you in a month. I love you, too." They hugged each other, and Lily turned to Kate. "Kate, nice meeting you."

"Yes, Lily, nice meeting you, too. Bon voyage!"

As Lily walked to the security line, Kate and Liam watched until she, too, disappeared into the terminal.

"Now she is gone," Liam said, looking a bit sad. Kate definitely understood how he felt.

"Yes, I just sent off my daughter and her boyfriend, too. They're going to Asia for seventeen whole days."

"Wow, that's exciting!"

"Yes."

"Kate, do you have a few minutes to grab coffee?"

She didn't think it was a good idea, but it would be rude to leave him. "Um… sure…"

"Good, let's sit down at the café over there."

Liam started walking toward the café, and Kate followed him. When they sat down with their coffee, Liam said, "I love the airport, don't you? It's great for people-watching."

"Yes, I do, too. It's like a real-life drama."

"I agree. Happy or sad, they are all here."

Kate added, "Plus, I love traveling, so I'm often part of those dramas."

"I love traveling, too…" But it was clear that Liam had something else on his mind, and sure enough, he said, "Kate, why don't you do lunch with me anymore?"

"Um… I have been so busy… you know, with the holidays."

"Okay, I understand that. But do you want to do lunch tomorrow?"

She hesitated. But she did like spending time with him—could they really be friends? Liam seemed like he still had expectations, but she didn't want to cut him out completely. "Um… maybe, I need to check my calendar. So, can I let you know later today?"

"That's fine. But do let me know, okay?" Kate nodded. They drank their coffee for a little while before Liam spoke again. "Are you still chatting with that man online?"

Kate was a little surprised. She hadn't thought Liam would remember. She searched for a good way to respond, but in the end she simply said yes.

"And did he say when he will come see you?"

"…No…"

"Kate… what are you going to do? You can't just keep talking to him online forever. That's not a real relationship."

Kate wished she could disagree. Her love for Edward felt real, but she truly longed to have him at her side. There was just no way to convince her mind the same way she could convince her heart. She admitted, "I know that. It's just that I don't know what to do anymore. I feel very comfortable when I talk to him, and he helps me get through the day…"

"I think it is very dangerous that you feel comfortable with him. It's a sign that he has succeeded in manipulating your emotions. The more you talk, the more you are sucked into his trap and the harder it is for you to get out…"

"… I understand what you are saying, but… I can't stop now."

"Why not? Just stop talking to him. He is not the only man out there–he may not even be a 'real' man. He could be a really advanced chatbot for all you know." Kate didn't respond. Liam continued, "Kate, you need to open your eyes. There are many men out there for you to meet. For instance, me."

Kate looked up at him, shocked. Liam grinned at her, as if he were joking. But then his smile fell. "On a serious note, Kate, I have been thinking a lot about you. I have to be honest– I want to start a serious relationship."

SEVENTEEN

A week had passed since Dominique and Tren left. They were probably in Cambodia by now, their second stop. Kate knew they'd planned to visit Tren's friends and relatives in Vietnam first, and that they were headed to Thailand after Cambodia. Dominique had sent Kate a few emails and many pictures from Vietnam. Kate had told her she and her friends wanted to go to Vietnam, too, and Dominique had been sure to tell her all about it. As she thought about her future trip, looking at those pictures, her phone rang.

It was Liam. Kate hesitated, wondering whether she should answer him. Liam's declaration at the airport had caught her completely off-guard. There must have been a truly stricken expression on her face, because Liam had quickly assured her he didn't need an answer and excused himself shortly after. Kate hadn't spoken to him since. She wasn't angry with him, or even particularly uncomfortable–but that realization, in turn, worried her. Had her heart become so fickle? Was she so desperate for love that she fell for anyone who gave her attention?

She couldn't even blame Liam for his skepticism. She was the one who couldn't defend Edward, not beyond "I trust him" and "I love him." Of course those would sound like excuses to someone who thought she was being scammed.

She picked up. "Hi Liam."

"Hi Kate. At least you answered my call." Liam's voice had a note of humor, which was good. "What are you doing, are you busy?"

"No, I was just looking at the pictures my daughter sent me from her trip."

"Did she like it there?"

"I really think so. She's still traveling, so I'll hear more from her when she gets back."

"Actually, I wanted to apologize for the other day at the airport. I think I was too direct."

"You don't have to apologize about that."

"Then, you accept my proposal?"

Quickly, Kate clarified, "Um, no, I didn't mean that way." She didn't want him to get his hopes too high just because her emotions were tangled up.

"I know, sorry. I am being direct again. We can go slowly, how's that?" Before Kate could reply, he pressed on, "Can we still go for lunch? You didn't call me after the airport the other day."

"Oh, I'm sorry." She'd completely forgotten that she'd promised to see him again soon. His confession had wiped everything else from her mind.

"It's okay. But will you say yes? It's only lunch and conversation, I promise."

Well, if he just wanted to talk… "When?"

"Tomorrow at noon, at your choice of restaurant."

Kate thought about it. She didn't want to go to a restaurant; it felt too much like a real date, and she wanted the freedom to leave whenever she wanted if she felt uncomfortable. "How about I make sandwiches, and we go to the park?"

"That's a terrific idea! Let's do that. A picnic in the park, how romantic!"

That wasn't what she meant, but she didn't have the heart to argue. It was true–she really did want to have a romantic picnic, but she'd been dreaming about it with Edward for months. "I'll meet you at San Mateo Central Park. I think the main entrance is on 5th Avenue."

"Got it, see you tomorrow."

****

The next day, Kate and Liam had a picnic in the park. After they met at the main gate, they walked around the park a little and found a picnic table by the pond, where they decided to have lunch. Liam placed Kate's picnic basket, which he carried from the car, on the table, and Kate opened it to reveal two sandwiches–Kate was pescatarian, but she'd made roast beef for Liam–two fruit cups, and two water bottles, along with napkins and utensils. They enjoyed their food in silence for a while, watching the ducks in the pond. Liam finally broke the silence. "This was such a great idea, a picnic in the park," he said, when he finished eating his sandwich.

"Yeah, I love doing it. I used to do a lot when my children were small," said Kate, trying to remember the good old days. "But I haven't done it for a long time. More than ten years."

"Why did you stop?"

"Oh, that was when I got divorced."

"Oh, I see…"

"Plus, teenagers don't enjoy this kind of stuff, right? Going on a picnic in the park with their parents."

"Right, they just want to hang out with their friends at the mall or something."

"Yeah. Sometimes I wish my kids wouldn't grow up, you know?"

"I know exactly what you mean. They grow up too fast, don't they? Before you know it, they're out of the house." Liam looked thoughtful for a few seconds, then continued, "But why did you suggest the picnic today?"

Kate shrugged awkwardly. She couldn't say she felt guilty, or that her mind still doubted Edward, even though she was working to trust him and follow her heart. She didn't want Liam to think she was pitying him, but she didn't want to encourage his feelings either. She came up with a lame excuse. "Oh, no special reason. I thought it would be a good change from eating at a restaurant. That's all."

She smiled at him, trying to camouflage her silly answer. Liam didn't look satisfied, but he let it go. Silence fell again, much less comfortable than before. Not for the first time, Kate doubted the wisdom of trying to hold onto this relationship. Liam moved onto his fruit, while Kate continued to eat her sandwich. Liam was clearly working up to saying something. A few bites of fruit, he finally asked her, "Kate, what are you thinking right now?"

Once again, his words took her by surprise; she couldn't respond immediately, at a loss for words. After several seconds of awkward silence, Kate decided to be straightforward. She said resolutely, "Um... Liam... I want to be honest with you, okay?"

"Okay."

"I was thinking about you and Edward, the man I have been chatting with online..."

"You were thinking of him and me?"

"Yes..."

"Why?"

"Well, um, because I have been in a 'relationship' with him, and yet I'm out with you. Even though you're just a friend, I can't help but think, what am I doing here? Is it morally right to be out with you like this? Stuff like that."

"Kate, that's what I like about you. You are truly a sincere and caring person. Putting aside my thoughts about that scammer guy… it's so kind of you to be considerate towards him."

"Thank you. I don't deserve that."

"Yes, you do. If you don't mind, I'd like to continue seeing you."

"Liam…" Kate looked at him. He gazed at her with open affection.

Wasn't this what she wanted? Someone to look at her in person and be by her side. Someone who openly cared about her, who listened to her and valued her. She wanted to be able to go on picnic dates or dine at restaurants, even travel together. Side by side.

But… she couldn't help it. She wanted those things with Edward.

"I like your company, Liam," she admitted. "But I don't want to use you as a replacement, and I won't betray Edward. I promised to trust him and have faith in him."

Liam leaned back. She expected him to look angry or disappointed, but he didn't. He looked patient and confident. "That's okay. I can wait until you give up on him, or he proves he's just scamming you. But in the meantime, can we keep spending time together?"

She should say no. But the voice in her head–the one that always sounded like Sara–reminded her of how many times Edward had failed to keep his promise, or given her odd, vague excuses. *What if Liam is right? Besides, Edward already knows about the blind date. Once he's here in person, you can talk about it then.* So, feeling a little guilty, she said, "Okay."

****

It was a fine day in Kuala Lumpur, even though it was the wet season. Dominique and Tren had arrived from Bangkok the night before–newly engaged, no less. Tren had proposed to her in Vietnam, and his family and friends had been ecstatic that she'd said yes. They'd both agreed early on that long engagements were the best, and Dominique was excited to spend the next few years growing even closer to her beloved. They planned to do some city sightseeing for their first day, and they had perfect weather for it.

Many tourists frolicked on the street, taking advantage of the nice weather. After breakfast, Dominique and Tren were ready to explore the city. Hats? Checked. Sunscreen? Checked. iPhones? Checked. Water? Checked. They were ready.

With the help of GPS and public transportation, they went all over the city. They visited Hindu temples and shrines, swung by Sunway Lagoon to cool off, then hit up Central Market for lunch. They went shopping around City Centre to see the futuristic Petronas Twin Towers, and after a quick jaunt back to their hotel, they headed out for dinner at a nearby local restaurant. The sun had just set, so it was still relatively bright, and the air was still very warm. As they approached the restaurant, they could smell the distinctive aroma of mixed spices. Tren liked spicy food more than Dominique did, but she enjoyed her food anyway.

When they came out, they saw a huge crowd in front of the restaurant. "Something must be going on. I wonder what?" Tren said. He started walking toward the crowd, and Dominique followed him. As they got closer, she saw it was a movie shoot. More and more people gathered around the curious crowd, and soon Dominique lost sight of Tren.

"Tren! Tren!" She called out his name, but there was no sign of him. It took some time to push her way out of the crowd; once she did, she walked around the perimeter, but she couldn't see Tren. The crowd had formed a thick circle around the actors and the set, and she could no longer get close enough to search for Tren.

"Where did he go?" she muttered. She looked at her phone and realized that it had less than 5% battery life. "Oh, no, and I didn't bring the charger. Damn it." After searching for a while in vain, she decided to walk back to the hotel.

After twenty minutes of walking, she realized that the hotel was nowhere near in sight. Even worse, her phone was completely dead. She was lost in a foreign country and she had no way of getting in touch with Tren. As she went around the corner, lost in thought, she bumped into someone. Startled, she screamed.

"Miss, are you okay?" The man looked concerned.

"Um, I'm okay. You speak English, can you please tell me how to get back to Hotel Lumpur? I think I'm lost."

"Yeah, you are definitely lost. This is not a good part of the city to walk around in, especially for a young girl like you alone at night. I can take you back to your hotel, but I have to swing by my house to do a few things. It's just down the street. Do you mind?"

Dominique immediately felt uncomfortable. "Um, I don't know... you can just show me the directions, and maybe I can manage myself..."

"I know what you're thinking, but I promise you don't have to worry about me. Trust me, you're way too young for me, haha."

Dominique was still hesitant, but the man seemed honest. "They say not to follow strangers, you know."

The man laughed. "You're right! But I don't want you to walk alone in this area. It will be a quick stop."

Well, what choice did she have? "Okay, but I'll wait for you outside."

"Okay, if you like."

Dominique followed the man for a couple of blocks. She knew her mother would be angry about her following a stranger, but somehow, she wasn't scared of him. His concern for her safety felt genuine. When they reached the house, he went inside, and Dominique waited outside the porch. It was a small house with a small front yard, but the yard was maintained nicely with lots of flowers in bloom, which reminded her of her own mother's garden. The man came back out after a little while.

"Okay, I'm ready to take you back to the hotel now. Ready?"

"Yes. Thanks for doing this."

"You're very welcome. I'm glad you bumped into me tonight, because there are quite a few dodgy people around here. What's your name?"

"Oh, I'm Dominique."

"That's a nice name. Nice meeting with you, Dominique. I'm Edward. Where are you from?"

Edward, huh? Wasn't that the name of her mom's internet boyfriend? Dominique couldn't remember. "California."

"Are you traveling by yourself?"

"Oh no, I was with my fiancé for dinner, but we got separated when we came out of the restaurant. I think there was a movie shoot going on, and there were so many people."

"Yeah, they do that a lot here. Your fiancé must be very worried."

"Yeah, my phone is dead, so I can't even call him or text him."

"Sorry, my cell phone can't call overseas numbers. Are you sure you don't want to use my house phone?"

"No, that's okay. Can you just take me back to the hotel?"

"Haha, okay. You're right, it's smart not to go inside a stranger's house. Where in California do you live?"

"I live in San Francisco with my fiancé."

"Oh, San Francisco. I'd love to visit that city someday." As they talked, Dominique realized she had fallen in step alongside Edward, instead of following behind him. She glanced at his face and noticed a thoughtful expression. "How far is it from there to Palo Alto?"

"To Palo Alto?" That was an oddly specific question. "Um, it takes about thirty minutes by car. Why? Do you know someone in Palo Alto?"

"My son is a student at Stanford University," Edward explained.

"Really, that's great. What year?"

"He's doing his third year of college there. A junior, I think you call it?"

"Right. What is he majoring in?"

"Software engineering."

"My fiancé is also an engineer," Dominique said. Her heart filled with pride as she thought about Tren.

"Wow, really?" That's amazing."

Dominique found herself warming up to Edward. He really sounded impressed and supportive. "What about you? What do you do here?"

"Oh–uh, I'm an engineer, too, actually. But it's not the same thing."

"You are, too? Wow! What's your son's name?"

"His name is Henrik."

"That's a nice name," Dominique said. "I know someone named Henrik too." A part of her was tempted to ask more about his son, but her mind was still filled with thoughts of getting back to Tren.

"Thanks." Edward smiled, but it disappeared quickly. "So, uh, where did you two visit today?"

Dominique wasn't sure why he wanted to change the subject, but she thought it was rude to ask. Instead, she told Edward about her visit to Batu Caves–the exhausting, 272-step climb, but the splendid panorama that awaited her and Tren at the top.

"Yeah, it's a great place for tourists. When I first arrived in this city, Batu Caves were the first thing I visited. Though, that was twenty years ago. It's probably different now."

"So you've been living here for twenty years?"

"Yeah, it's been too long…"

"Where are you originally from?"

"I'm from Iceland. I was taking a gap year, actually, and I decided to explore Southeast Asia. I went to Thailand and Cambodia before I ended up here."

"Oh, Tren and I flew from Bangkok yesterday. We visited Vietnam and Cambodia before that."

"That's great," Edward said. His voice sounded warm and kind. "Did you have fun?"

"Yeah, we did."

They continued to talk as Edward led her back to the hotel. By the time they reached an area Dominique recognized, she felt as though they were good friends. Edward was a good conversationalist. Before they reached the hotel, Edward asked her if he could swing into a nearby convenience store; Dominique agreed. She bought two bottles of water and some snacks, while Edward bought a pack of cigarettes.

"You smoke?" she asked, as they left the store.

"Unfortunately, yes. I'm trying to quit, though. When I leave here, I'll quit for good."

"Are you leaving soon?" Dominique thought he would be disappointed, but instead, he nodded eagerly.

"I really hope so, I don't know when I can leave, though."

"Are you going back to Iceland?"

"I eventually will, but I plan to go to Stanford to see my son and stay there for a while."

"Really? We might be neighbors, then! Or, well, my mom lives in Palo Alto, so you might be her neighbor."

"Your mother lives in Palo Alto?"

"Yeah, with my grandmother."

"What kind of town is Palo Alto?"

"It's pretty nice. It's right next to Stanford, so it's a college town."

"Hmmm…" Dominique couldn't read the look on Edward's face, but when he spoke again, he sounded wistful. "Sounds nice."

Silence fell between them as they approached the hotel. Eventually, Dominique ventured, "Are you okay, Edward? You got awfully quiet."

"Oh, I'm okay. Sorry, I was just thinking about–" Edward started, then paused. "--uh, my son."

That made sense. "You and his mom must miss him a lot," she said. Edward smiled awkwardly.

"Actually, I don't know where his mom is. She left one day, and… I just never saw her again."

"Oh, I'm sorry," Dominique said sincerely. "Was she Icelandic too?"

"No, she's Malaysian."

"I see." That meant his son was half. Something about that seemed important, but then they reached the hotel lobby, and she was distracted by thoughts of Tren again. She turned to Edward and clapped her hands in front of her. "Thank you so much! I don't know how I would have survived tonight without you."

"You're very welcome. Don't get separated from your fiancé anymore, okay?"

"Okay." But Dominique didn't want to leave him with lonely, melancholy thoughts, not after he had been so nice. She dug a piece of paper and a pen out of her purse, then jotted down her email address. "Um, when you come to Stanford, maybe you can contact me, if you like. My mom and I can show you around, if you want–I mean, your son can too, but…"

Edward saved her from her awkwardness. "I'd like that very much. Thanks!"

"Welcome. Good night, Edward, thanks again."

"Good night, Dominique. Take care."

She quickly made her way back to the hotel room. When she opened the room door, Tren came running to her. He looked so relieved to see her and hugged her immediately.

"Oh, Dominique, I'm so glad you are back. I've been trying to call you and text you for the last hour."

"Sorry, my phone died five minutes after we got separated, and I got lost. A nice man brought me back to the hotel."

"A man walked you back to the hotel?"

"Yeah, I bumped into him and asked him for directions, because he spoke English. But he said I got lost in the shady part of the city, so he escorted me all the way here."

"You were lucky, what if he was a predator himself?"

Dominique shook her head reassuringly. "I worried about that too, but he was a perfect gentleman. Oh, yeah, he said his son, named Henrik, is an engineering major at Stanford. He also said that he hopes to come see him soon and stay in Palo Alto for a while. But he doesn't know anyone there besides his son, and his wife–or, I guess she was his wife? I don't know– isn't around anymore, so I gave him my email address."

"You what? You gave a stranger your email address? Oh, Dominique…" Tren looked a little amazed.

"Only my email address, no phone number or mailing address. It should be fine. Besides, I'm telling you he is a good person."

Tren's brow furrowed suddenly, as if a thought had just occurred to him. "Hey, Dominique, isn't Henrik majoring in engineering? Mike's friend? He's from Malaysia, I remember."

Dominique gasped. "You're right, Tren! I didn't even think about that. This means the person I bumped into tonight might be Henrik's father! What a small world!"

"We'll have to ask him about it when we get back." Tren hugged her. "For now, I'm just glad you're safe."

Over the next two days, they did more sightseeing and bought a lot of souvenirs. They were careful not to get separated again. Dominique was hoping to run into Edward again, but she did not. After four days, Dominique and Tren flew back to California.

EIGHTEEN

"Hey Henrik!" Mike stuck his head into Henrik's dorm room. "Can I come in?"

"Yeah, c'mon in. What's up?"

"Oh, not much. Just taking a break from studying."

"Oh, I need one too," Henrik said, as he put down the textbook he was reading.

School would be out in two weeks, but before they could enjoy some time off, the students had to go through a week of finals. Many students went to the library to study, Henrik's roommate included; Henrik, however, preferred to study in private, so he had the whole room to himself until midnight.

"Are you ready for the finals?" Mike asked as he shut the door and moved to sit down.

Henrik shrugged. "Not really, but I'll do my best. Are you ready, Mike?"

"Nah, never." Both boys laughed.

"What's your plan for Christmas and New Year's, Henrik?"

"I have no plans."

"Aren't you going back to Malaysia?"

"No, I don't think so."

"Is your dad coming to see you, then?"

"I don't know. He hasn't said anything." Henrik tried to keep his voice light.

"Hmmm… If you stay here over the winter recess, we can go to Lake Tahoe for skiing. Have you ever skied before?"

"Yeah, I have."

"Does it snow in Malaysia?"

"No, not really. I skied in Iceland. My grandparents live there."

"Oh, really? Cool! I always wanted to ski in that part of the world, in cold countries, you know. But yeah, what do you think?"

"Skiing at Lake Tahoe sounds great!"

"Great! We have a little cottage up there."

As they talked, Mike started spinning in the desk chair. Henrik looked at his friend's childish behavior and shook his head, laughing. He then picked up a notebook to write something down.

"This is fun. You should try it sometime," Mike called, still spinning. Henrik waved a dismissive hand and ignored the sounds of movement until Mike spoke again.

"Hey, you never told me you had a girlfriend. Who is she? Where did you meet her?"

"What are you talking about? I don't have a girlfriend. I would have told you."

"Then, what's this letter addressed to Kate Fleming?"

Henrik looked up from his notebook and saw Mike holding the letter. He jumped up and grabbed the letter out of Mike's hand in one motion. Mike looked stunned.

"Whoa! What was that about? You don't need to be shy about it. It's kind of romantic to write a letter to someone, I think."

"I didn't write this letter. My dad did. Remember when I first met you at the café, I told you I was looking for someone?"

"Yeah, I remember. So, that's who you are looking for?"

"Yeah."

"Is she your dad's girlfriend?"

"I think so, but I'm not sure."

Mike hummed thoughtfully. "So you still haven't found her yet."

"No, and I don't know how to find her. Plus, I can't spare any time right now for this letter."

"Right. We've got finals next week… Well, I'm gonna go back to my room and study for a few more hours. See ya later."

"Okay, see ya."

As Mike left, Henrik looked at the letter in his hand. Soon, he put it back and resumed his writing.

****

Two days after Dominique and Tren returned home from their Southeast Asian trip, they came over to Kate's house. William and Laura had been back for two days, and Kate had invited her three friends over for dinner; thus, the night promised to be a delightful one with so many people. Kate cooked mustard salmon and lemon chicken with roasted vegetables, cauliflower soup, and bean salad, while Jane brought pecan pie and Sara brought wine. Dominique and Tren particularly appreciated Kate's home cooking after eating spicy foods overseas during their vacation.

After an exchange of pleasantries, everybody asked the young couple about their recent trip to Southeast Asia. Kate already knew some of the details from Dominique's emails, but much of what Tren and Dominique described was new to her, too–including Dominique's story about getting lost. When

Dominique finished, Jane spoke excitedly, "Wow, Dominique, what an experience! And you were absolutely okay?"

"Yeah, here I am, very much alive!" She smiled, but she looked a little nervous–and for good reason, as Kate shook her finger at her daughter.

"You were just lucky, Dominique! But don't ever do that again!" she scolded seriously.

"I know, I know. I'll never get lost again. I'll use one of those baby leashes attached to me and Tren, how's that?" Everybody burst into laughter. Even Kate laughed; as a mother, of course she was worried, but Dominique was sitting there safe and sound, so she couldn't be too upset.

"That's a splendid idea, Dom!" Sara said, still laughing. Once she stopped, she said thoughtfully, "You know, isn't that a weird coincidence that you met a guy named Edward, whose son is studying engineering at Stanford?" The room fell quiet, and Sara continued, "Jane, Mike's friend–the boy who stayed with you over summer, he's an engineering major from Malaysia, isn't he?"

"Henrik? I believe so. Let me text Mike," Jane said. She pulled out her phone and began to type.

"Do you know his dad's name?"

"No, do you want me to ask? Mike should be with him, they're supposed to be studying."

"Yeah, please."

Kate shook her head. She knew where this was going. "Sara Forster, playing detective? Even if the Edward Dominique met in Kuala Lumpur is Henrik's father, there is nothing that connects it to my Edward." Sara gave her a knowing look at the words "My Edward," and Kate blushed, but she continued, "My Edward is in London. How do you explain that, huh?"

"Yeah, how?" Mary chimed in. "Unless…"

"Unless what?" Jane spoke this time.

"Unless Kate's Edward is lying… let's think hypothetically for a moment. Let's just say for the sake of argument that Kate's Edward has actually lived in Malaysia for the last twenty years. Kate, what's your Edward's son's name?"

"Henrik," Kate said, then added quickly, "But I think that's pretty common, just like Edward."

"And what's he studying in college?"

Kate frowned, thinking back over her conversations with Edward. "…Engineering," she said slowly. Sara nodded, looking determined; a quick glance around the table showed that everyone else was drawn in, too.

"So he has a son named Henrik, a college student who's studying engineering–"

"In Iceland," Kate interrupted.

"--supposedly in Iceland," Sara continued. "Our Henrik is from Malaysia, but he's majoring in engineering, and his dad's name is Edward. Dominique met Edward in Kuala Lumpur, and he has a son who is majoring in engineering at Stanford."

"Wait!" Dominique said suddenly. "The Edward I met–he said he's from Iceland! And he mentioned that his son's mom left! And–"

Tren caught on. "Didn't Henrik say at Thanksgiving that his mom left when he was a baby?"

"Exactly!"

Sara nodded, satisfied with her deductive reasoning. "I definitely think that Kate's Edward is lying. He's been lying to you all these months that he is based in London. In fact, he is based in Kuala Lumpur and is possibly a scammer. Through some crazy stroke of fate, Dominique ran into him. That's my conclusion."

Everybody looked speechless. Even though most of them

had already said similar things to Kate in private, nobody wanted to believe it for certain, let alone say it out loud.

"That means Henrik's father is a conman?" asked Tren sheepishly.

"Unfortunately, yes," Mary confirmed.

"Wait a second, everybody," Kate cried. "Henrik is a very sweet boy! He insisted on cleaning up at Thanksgiving, and Mike wouldn't still be friends with him if Henrik was suspicious or a bad kid. He is absolutely not a son of a conman. This is all just a crazy hypothesis. Not the truth…"

"Maybe he doesn't know what his dad does," William cut in.

"But–like I said, Edward isn't in Malaysia. He's in London. And his son doesn't go to Stanford, and–oh! And I remember, he said his son is half-Greek! And his wife only passed away four years ago."

"How do you know that for sure? Because he told you, right?" Sara asked, looking skeptical.

"Um, yes…" Kate couldn't go on.

"He probably lied so that you can't track him down after he steals your money and runs off."

Mary nodded. "The only things that break all the connecting dots are 'London,' 'Stanford,' and 'Greek.' And those are all things he told you, Kate."

There was a heavy silence after Mary's last words. Kate's head was spinning; she had no idea what to think, or how to feel. Then, a chime sounded from Jane's phone.

"Mike just texted me back. Henrik's dad's name is Edward."

"Can you ask him for more details? Like how long he's been living in Malaysia?" asked Mary.

"And where he's from, if he wasn't born there," Sara added, and Mary nodded.

"Sure." Jane typed in more messages. Another chime was heard much quicker this time. Jane gasped, cupping her mouth with her hand. "Oh my god!"

"What?" Sara demanded. Kate didn't say anything, her heart pounding in her chest. She wasn't sure she wanted to know what Jane was about to say.

"He's lived in Malaysia for the last twenty years. He's originally from Iceland!"

Dominique bounced in her chair, excited. "Mom! It's actually him!"

"Kate, what's your Edward's last name? And Henrik's?" Mary asked. Kate blinked, feeling faint.

"Edward's last name is Jónsson, with an accent on the first 'o'... I don't remember Henrik's. I think I saw it in the very beginning... Ah..."

"Wait a minute. I think I saw 'my' Edward's last name when we went to his house," Dominique interrupted. "Where did I see it?... Ah, ah, oh yeah, I saw it on the mailbox as we left his house there. I think it was the same!"

Everybody was completely speechless. They looked at each other but did not utter any words. Then, Sara asked Jane to confirm Henrik's dad's last name. Jane typed in the message. A reply came in almost instantly.

"Henrik's dad's last name is Jónsson with an accent on the first 'o'!"

"Oh my god," Dominique said, shaking Tren's hand in excitement. Kate watched the action numbly, feeling as though she'd left her body entirely. She could barely process what was happening.

"I think we need to write down all the moving pieces on a piece of paper, so we can see the connection more clearly. Kate, do you have a whiteboard or something?" asked Mary.

"I'll get them," William said quickly. He jumped from the chair and ran upstairs, leaving the others to chat excitedly about everything they'd just learned. Sara squeezed Kate's shoulder, and Kate mustered up a smile for her, even though she didn't quite feel it. Was she happy? Upset? It was impossible to tell–she was simply shocked. Soon, William came back with an easel and the whiteboard. He placed them in the center of the room so that everyone could see.

"Now," Sara began, "Let me write down all the moving pieces here." She divided the whiteboard in three sections and wrote the different "Edwards" at the top of each column. Then she wrote all the facts underneath each heading.

	Dominique's Edward	Henrik's Edward	Kate's Edward
Name	Edward Jónsson	Edward Jónsson	Edward Jónsson
Home country	Iceland	Iceland	Iceland
Profession	Engineer	Engineer	Engineer (scammer?)
Length of time in current country	Malaysia for 20 years	Malaysia for 20 years	England for 20 years
Son	Henrik Edwardsson	Henrik Edwardsson	Henrik XXXXXX
Son's college	Stanford	Stanford	A college in Iceland
Major	Engineering	Engineering	Engineering (probably)
Henrik's mom	Malaysian, left when he was a baby	Malaysian, left when he was a baby	Greek, died four years ago (supposedly)

"There is no doubt that the Edward Dominique met is Henrik's father," said Mary triumphantly, pointing at the first two columns in the table. "Though we don't know much about the son of Kate's Edward, I suspect that the Henrik we know is his son. Thus, all three Edwards are the same person."

A murmur ran through the room. Kate grasped for something, anything to disprove the theory. She wasn't even entirely sure why she was fighting so hard–it was, after all, better for her to know the truth, and Henrik was a tangible connection to the love of her life. Perhaps it was a deep-seated need to believe that Henrik hadn't lied to her. Laura, who had been quietly listening to the conversation the whole time, suddenly spoke up. "How come Edward and Henrik have different last names?"

Everyone grudgingly agreed that was a good point; except Sara, who was determined to stick with her theory. "Jane, do you mind sending Mike one more message? Ask him why Henrik has a different last name from his dad."

"Of course."

They waited in tense silence. After fifteen minutes, a chime finally came in. Jane looked at the message and cupped her mouth once again.

"He said Iceland has a unique naming system, and parents and children usually don't have the same last name… then he said to google it if we wanted to know the reason, because they have to study," she said, fanning her face.

"Can someone google it?" asked Mary.

"I'll do it," William volunteered. He pulled out his own phone and typed, then started reading aloud. "In Iceland, the boy's last name is determined by his father's first name plus 'son,' meaning son. For example, if the father's first name is Jón, his son's last name will be Jónsson, literally meaning Jón's son. A girl's last name is determined by her father's first name plus 'dóttir,' meaning daughter…"

"That's enough, William, thanks," Sara interrupted.

"Right," William said, looking a little flushed. He put his phone away.

"Now we know why Henrik doesn't have the same last name as Edward," Mary said.

"But still, there is no hard evidence that my Edward is Henrik's father…" Kate protested.

Sara turned to Kate and said warmly, "Kate dear, we are not trying to hurt you, though I think that's been inevitable for a while. We are only trying to help you see the truth. Edward has been lying to you all these months. I'm so surprised that you haven't sent him any money yet."

Kate said nothing.

"We have to connect the first two Edwards to Kate's Edward," Mary said. "I think we need to know a bit more about the son of Kate's Edward. Kate, can you ask him tonight? Maybe you can get some more specific details, or catch him in a lie or something." She paused, then looked a little embarrassed, as if she'd just realized how pushy she sounded. "I know it must be hard to accept all of this, but we are all concerned about you. I think you need to get to the bottom of it and forget about him once and for all, if he is scamming you."

"… Um, I don't know… maybe. But I just can't believe that Edward has been lying all along. Of course I never completely dismissed the thought of him scamming me, but I chose to believe him and trust him. Most of all, I love him." Kate was embarrassed to discover she was almost in tears. Immediately, the atmosphere of the room changed, and Sara's tone shifted.

"Alright, we've done enough for now. We should give Kate time and space." Everybody nodded in agreement. They cleared the table and started to get ready to leave. Dominique, Tren, Jane and Mary picked up their things and headed to the door, thanking Kate for dinner. William and Laura went upstairs. Kate was left alone with Sara in the living room.

"Do you want me to stay with you tonight?" Sara offered.

"No, I'm okay. You can go. I need to think about this whole thing alone."

"Okay, if you say so, but if you need me, call me."

"I will." Kate smiled weakly. "Thanks for your concern. I love you."

"I love you, too. Talk to you tomorrow?"

"Yes, talk to you tomorrow."

They hugged each other, and Sara left, leaving Kate all alone. As soon as Sara was out the door, Kate ran up to her bedroom and threw herself onto the bed, then cried quietly for a long time.

****

Henrik and Mike sat in Mike's dorm room, talking about the series of questions Jane had asked them. Henrik was very curious about why she wanted to know so much about him. Mike had texted his mother after they'd finished studying and was reading the long reply he'd just received.

"My mom said Dominique met a guy named Edward in Kuala Lumpur, and they think he was probably your dad," explained Mike. "Also, Kate has some online boyfriend who's also named Edward, and his son's name is Henrik too. So, they are trying to see if it's all the same guy."

"Dominique ran into my dad? That's crazy! Kuala Lumpur is huge, what a coincidence." Then, the rest of what Mike said caught up to him. "Wait, you said they think Kate has been talking to my dad online?!"

"Yeah–well, no, they're not sure, actually. They need a bit more information about his son."

"Mike–the letter! My dad is looking for someone named

Kate around Palo Alto! …Oh, but wait, he's looking for a 'Kate Fleming.'" Henrik's hope died quickly, but Mike looked at him with wide eyes.

"What?! Wait a minute! Kate Fleming?! That's her! That's aunt Kate's name!"

"What?! She said her name was Kate Smith!"

"Yeah, Smith's her maiden name. She just recently changed it back, my mom said. Sorry I didn't think of it earlier, I was completely preoccupied with finals." Mike grabbed his shoulder and shook. "Do you get it? We found her! It's gotta be your dad's Kate!"

"Are you kidding?! She's been here right under my nose all these months?!"

"We've gotta tell her right now!"

"Yeah!" Henrik looked at the clock; it was already midnight. "Ugh! It's too late now, she's probably asleep already. I'll text her first thing in the morning."

"Yeah. Good night, and congrats, man!"

"Haha, don't say that just yet. Night."

****

Once her tears dried up, Kate sat on her bed. She had felt devastation a few times with Edward, but this was the final blow. Every fact her family and friends found led to one conclusion: Edward had majorly lied to her from the start. He was most likely a true conman, and his sweet, polite son probably didn't even know it.

She thought about her first encounter with Henrik. He'd seemed so familiar, but she couldn't quite figure out why, but now it was very clear. She had looked at his son's profile once before, back in the beginning. It was there that she'd seen an old picture of him, and his last name; she'd forgotten quickly, because the account was clearly rarely used. In person and older, his resemblance to his father was obvious. Well, at least that means he didn't use a fake photo, Kate thought. Then she buried her face in her hands.

"I'm such a fool, a complete fool," she sighed. The worst part was, even though the result was nothing but heartbreak and lies, she didn't feel like she had wasted the last ten months. She and Edward had created a special and magical world in which they both felt comfortable existing. They couldn't touch or hear each other; they'd only had written words to exchange. But Edward had always put her at ease. He'd made her feel seen, heard, loved. He'd reminded her of all the things she loved to do. He'd brought beauty and love back into her life.

She was heartbroken—there was no doubt about that. Even as she gazed unseeingly at the wall, she could feel the deep urge to cry all over again. But it wasn't the same as it had been after he asked her for money. But this was different, because there was no coming back from Edward's lies. She would have to take the wonderful memories with her and move on.

She opened her Facebook account and expected to see a message from Edward, but to her surprise, there was none. She started typing in her message, her last message.

> Hi Edward, how are you? How was your night? Hope it was fine...

> How is your son? You told me about him before, but I kind of forgot, so tell me again.

> What is his full name? Where is he going to college? And what is he majoring in?

What does he want to be after
he graduates? Will I meet him soon,
too?

Sorry about so many
questions.

Well, looks like you are not
there, so I'll be back later.

The last sentence was a lie. She would not be coming back to this chat ever again. She looked at her messages vacantly for several seconds and then got up with determination. She picked up her phone and tapped Liam's name. On the second ring, he answered, "Hello, Kate?"

"Yes, it is. Sorry to call you so late."

"It's fine. Are you okay?"

"Yeah, sorry to worry you. I was just wondering if you would like to have dinner with me tomorrow night."

"Dinner, really? We are finally moving from lunch to dinner?"

"Yes. Is that a problem?" Kate asked hesitantly.

"No, no problem at all. I'll pick you up at seven. Is that okay?"

"Yes, that's fine. See you tomorrow, and good night."

"Yeah, see you tomorrow. Good night."

Kate hung up and squared her shoulders. "There, I'm moving on."

NINETEEN

For five days, Edward had been thinking about Dominique and the conversation he'd had with her. She had said that her mother was half-Japanese and half-white, was born in Japan and lived there until after her college graduation, and had been living in the U.S. for the past twenty years. She lived in Palo Alto, as did Dominique's grandmother. Other details, too, jumped out as strangely familiar. But to Edward, the key was Dominique's resemblance to Kate.

Her name had caught his attention at the time, but he'd thought he was simply being delusional, longing to be by Kate's side so much that he was projecting onto random strangers. Plus, he'd been distracted, half his thoughts on figuring out how to get around Aidan's ultimatum. But looking back on it, he was almost certain that Dominique was Kate's daughter. "I should've asked her about her mother's name," Edward mumbled, kicking himself.

Then something clicked in his mind. Tren probably wasn't a common name in America; he could ask Kate if her daughter had a fiancé named Tren, as subtly as he could manage. Then, he would find a way to secretly email Dominique and explain his situation. It wasn't much, but maybe it would ease Kate's heart until he could escape Malaysia and go to her.

With these thoughts, Edward felt very hopeful. There was still no news from Henrik, but Edward believed that he would find her soon.

Edward was two blocks away from his office when he saw smoke rising into the sky. As he got closer, he saw flames. He ran to the last block to find out that it was his office building on fire. There was a big crowd gathered in front of the burning building. He was speechless, but managed to ask someone who was standing next to him, "Do you know how the fire started? Did everyone get out?"

"I think so," the man answered, ignoring Edward's first question.

"Are you sure? Where are they?"

Edward looked around, and it was then that he heard someone calling his name. He looked in the direction of the voice and saw a bunch of his coworkers. As he reached them, Edward felt relief–even if they weren't close, he was glad they were okay. But soon, one of them shouted at him, "Aidan is still inside the building!"

"What?! Aidan is still in there?!"

"We saw him come in earlier, but we thought he'd left! But his car is still in the parking lot, and he hasn't come out yet!"

Edward didn't stop to think before he dashed toward the building. He knew the layout and all the shortcuts, so it didn't take him long to get to the office. As he dodged his way through the raging fire, he spotted many things burning through the smoke: computers, file cabinets, desks, and everything else that Edward had been using since he began working for Aidan. He felt like the past twenty years were crumbling to dust. But there was no time for reflection. He had to find Aidan.

"Aidan! Aidan! Where are you? Can you hear me? Aidan!" Dodging the flames, Edward moved quickly around the office, but Aidan was nowhere to be seen. He looked inside Aidan's office and the restroom to no avail. He then opened the door to the fire escape and saw a figure on the walkway. It was Aidan, trapped under two burning beams that fell on top of him. "Aidan! Are you okay? Aidan!"

Aidan moaned, so quietly that Edward could barely hear him. Driven by adrenaline, Edward leapt into action. He tried to move the top beam, but it wouldn't budge. He tried again, and this time it moved slightly. With every ounce of strength he had, he tried one more time; this time, it moved enough for him to reach the bottom beam. The flames were getting stronger and stronger by the minute.

Then, he heard the fire engine. He ran to the fire escape landing and waved at the firefighters. "Over here," he screamed. "There is someone trapped here! Come quick!"

A few firefighters quickly climbed up the fire escape ladders, and soon they reached the level where Edward was standing. Edward pointed toward Aidan, and the firefighters took over. While two firefighters lifted the second beam, the third firefighter pulled Aidan out and carried him down. One more escorted Edward safely back to the ground, promising that his "friend" would be okay. Once he got to a safe place, he stopped and looked at Aidan, who was being carried on a gurney into the ambulance.

"Aidan!" Edward shouted, running toward him. "Will he be okay? Can I go with him to the hospital?" A paramedic said there was no need, as Aidan most likely would sleep through the night from medication. She added that it would be best to go home and rest, then come back in the morning. She then patted Edward's shoulder, saying that he did good. They treated him for smoke inhalation and a slight cut on the arm. After the ambulance zoomed off, Edward stood there, watching the firefighters work. In half an hour, the fire was completely contained, and the spectators started to disperse. In the end, Edward was the only one standing there. His mind was blank with shock. Noticing he was alone, he turned and started to walk home, feeling numb.

****

Kate woke up an hour later than usual, still exhausted from all the crying she'd done the night before. She picked up her phone from the side table and found a couple of messages: One was from her mother, and the other was from Henrik, who claimed he needed to see her right away. *Is he in on Edward's scam?* No, that was uncharitable. Henrik had only ever been sweet and polite. Still, whatever it was he had to say, Kate didn't really want to hear it. She was tired of her heart getting jerked around.

Henrik sent her a few more messages throughout the day, but she dismissed them all, focusing on work and chores. When it was time to get ready for her date, she showered, did her hair and light makeup, then put on a black dress, gold earrings, and a gold bracelet. She looked at herself in the mirror and nodded, satisfied. Then, she added a blue-green wool jacket and a matching purse. *There, I'm ready.* She supposed she should feel nervous, or excited, or even heartbroken still. Instead, she just felt distant.

She only had about fifteen minutes to wait before the doorbell rang. She went to the front door to open it and saw Liam standing there with a big smile.

"Hi, Kate. Are you ready?"

"Hi, Liam. Yes, I am. Let's go."

****

The main course went well. Kate and Liam chatted amicably;

Liam didn't push her to talk about her sudden urge to go on a date, but eventually, the topic came out anyway. As they ate, Kate explained everything she and her friends had learned; Liam seemed shocked, which was good. It meant Sara probably hadn't said anything to Eric, at least not yet. The waiter returned to take their dessert order, but Kate didn't want any, so she only ordered a cappuccino. Liam did the same.

After the waiter left, Liam turned to Kate, still trying to process what he had heard. He finally said, "What a story. I'm sorry that it turned out this way, Kate… but I believe it is all for the better. I'm just so glad that he didn't get your money after all."

"Thanks, you are very kind. I feel like I just woke up from a long dream. Now I can move on."

"Are you ready to move on… with me?"

"Yes, I am," Kate said firmly. "That's why I asked you to have dinner with me tonight."

Liam took Kate's hand and caressed it gently. His warm hands felt good on her cold ones. She noticed him looking at her lips, but he didn't lean in to kiss her; inwardly, she was grateful. The waiter returned with the check. As Kate reached to grab it, Liam grabbed it a second faster. "I got it."

"Oh no, it is my treat, since I asked," Kate contested.

"No, it is my treat to celebrate your new start," Liam said, and threw a quick wink at Kate. She smiled at him, and he smiled back at her. They were quiet as they paid and left the restaurant, and on the drive back to Kate's house. Kate's thoughts were on what would happen once they arrived, and it seemed Liam's were too.

He walked her to the front door, where she hesitated. Steeling herself, she asked, "Would you like to come in for a nightcap?"

"I'd love to, but are you sure?"

"Yes, I'm sure."

Kate opened the door, and Liam followed her in. She motioned for him to go to the living room to sit down while she got drinks. As she turned toward the kitchen, Liam grabbed her arm and pulled her close to him. She knew what was about to happen. She looked at him and nodded slightly. Without losing a second, Liam pulled her even closer and kissed her gently on the lips. She returned it with equal gentleness. They held each other, kissing and caressing.

Kate didn't know how much time passed, but Liam's kisses got rougher and more passionate. Kate tried to respond, but something snapped inside her. She suddenly pulled herself away from him and said very quietly, "Oh, Liam, I'm sorry, I can't do this. I'm so sorry."

Liam looked at her, confused. "Why? Don't be scared."

"No, I'm not scared... I don't think I'm ready... I'm so sorry..."

"You're not ready...?"

"I thought I was, but no, I'm not ready yet... please forgive me. Please leave now."

Liam stared at her, but he seemed to sense that she was serious. He opened the door and left quietly.

****

When Edward reached home, he felt like every bone in his body was crumbling down. He was dead tired. He couldn't get the image of Aidan, trapped under the burning beams, out of his mind. Maybe it was foolish in the long run to rescue the man who had ruined his life, but Edward hadn't been thinking like that in the moment. He had heard someone needed rescuing and moved on autopilot.

He went to grab a beer from the fridge, but a piece of paper stuck to the front caught his eye: Dominique's email address. Suddenly, everything he'd been thinking about before the fire came flooding back. Dominique, Kate–his opportunity, at long last, to get his letter to her for sure.

If he was going to contact her, now would be the time to do it. As soon as he thought it, he felt an odd kind of guilt; maybe it was terrible or selfish to think about his escape when Aidan was in the hospital. It wasn't like Edward liked him, but he'd always appreciated everything Aidan had done for Henrik. And besides that, after so many years, it was impossible not to care about Aidan in some ways. Edward didn't think their relationship could be defined in simple terms anymore.

But it was probably now or never. So, moving carefully and trying to keep his breathing steady, he moved to his laptop and pulled up his email. He typed in Dominique's email address, then began typing his message:

Dear Dominique,

How are you? This is Edward, Edward Jónsson from Kuala Lumpur, Malaysia. Remember the old man you bumped into when you got lost, who took you back to your hotel? We chatted on the way back, and something you told me stuck in my mind ever since. It is about your mother. I have a very good reason to believe that she and I have been chatting online for almost a year. I can explain everything in more detail when I am there in California. But right now, let me get straight to the point: Please find my son, Henrik Edwardsson at Stanford, and tell him that I've found her. So, all he has to do is to deliver the letter to your mother. Please also tell her to ignore my request at the end of the letter, and to wait for me a little longer. It's not important anymore.

Dominique, this is very important for her and me, so please act immediately. Then, I'll be grateful to you for the rest of my life.

Yours sincerely,
Edward
   P.S. I'm already grateful that you gave me your email address,
which I'm putting to use much sooner than I expected.

TWENTY

"Mom, the front door is left open!" Dominique shouted. Kate, who had been sitting on the sofa in the living room, crying, looked up to find Dominique flanked by Henrik and Tren.

She quickly wiped off her tears and said, "Oh, hi Tren, hi Henrik."

"Mom, why was the front door open? And who was that man who just left?"

"Oh, you saw him? He is just a friend…"

"Why didn't you turn the light on? What's going on?" Dominique moved closer to Kate, and Kate saw her eyes widen. "Mom, were you crying?"

"No, it's nothing. I'm okay now. What are you three doing here?"

"Right. Mom, listen. I got an email from Edward, and– look, Henrik has something for you, and it's really important." Dominique turned to Henrik and urged, "Henrik, show it to her." Henrik nodded solemnly.

"Kate. I believe this is for you." He held out a white envelope addressed to *Kate Fleming*. She got up and took it from Henrik, staring at her own name. She then turned the envelope over and saw: *Edward Jónsson*.

"Edward Jónsson," Kate murmured faintly.

"Yes, he is my father, and he asked me to deliver this letter to you," Henrik said quietly but firmly, as Dominique and Tren looked on.

"Let's go sit down at the table," Kate said faintly. She walked into the dining room, followed by the kids. Kate and Henrik sat down next to each other on one side, and Tren moved to sit down on the other side, but Dominique quickly said, "Mom, perhaps we should leave you two alone."

Kate shook her head. "No, please stay. I want you to be here while I read this." The couple looked at each other, then sat down across from her and Henrik. Then, the front door opened; Kate heard William and Laura call out that they were back, and soon they, too, walked into the dining room.

"What's going on? Everybody looks so serious," exclaimed William. Dominique shushed her brother, but Kate shook her head again, this time reassuringly.

"William, Laura, you two can sit down, too." Kate motioned them quietly. They sat down next to Dominique and Tren. Kate looked at each one of them and nodded at Henrik. She then slowly opened the envelope and started reading the letter.

May 27, 2018

My Dearest Kate,

Before you start reading this letter, I want you to know that the boy who is delivering it is my son, Henrik. And please ask him to stay with you, while you read it. Or you can read it together with him, as it concerns him a great deal, too.

Well, where to begin? I suppose I get straight to the point, as I don't want to tell you another lie as long as I live. We have been chatting online for almost four months, and half of the stuff I've told you is a lie. The truth is, your suspicions about me have always been correct. I work as a romance scammer in Malaysia. I reach out to women around the world and earn their trust. Once I receive money from them, I move on. I have been in this line of work for the last 20 years.

I'm sure you're horrified by me right now, and I don't blame you. I know this is a disgusting job, and I promise you, I hate it too. I'll understand if you never want to speak to me again. I only ask that you finish reading this letter, and that you tell me your thoughts. My future depends on you.

Now let me tell you how I got into this pathetic situation. After graduating from high school in Iceland, I wanted to take some time off and travel around the world. I landed in Malaysia last. I was only going to stay here for a few days, as I was running out of the funds to travel further. On the last day, I was drinking at a small bar, when some locals came up and asked me to join a drinking contest against a girl. She said if she won, I would have to go with her. I casually said okay, thinking that she would never win. But I was wrong, and... well. When I woke up the next morning, I was in her bed, with no memory of how I got there. I don't know if they spiked the drinks, or if she could just really hold her liquor...

That's not the point. To make a long story short, she turned out to be someone's wife, and he was furious. Turns out, you can get arrested for adultery in Malaysia, did you know that? And maybe the courts would've gone easy on me as a foreigner, but Aidan—that's the man, my boss—is so powerful here, I can't even tell you how much. Plus, I was a dumb, terrified kid. So when he said he wouldn't press charges if I paid him off, I wanted to agree— but I was broke. So he said I could work for him until I earned $5,000.

Aidan got me an apartment close to his office so that I could walk to work, and so he could keep an eye on me to make sure I didn't try to run back to Iceland. In the office, he taught me how to be a scammer–he has a script and a list of names and everything, which is how I found your profile. (I don't know how or why he picked you, but I'm honestly glad I got to meet you, even if it was like this.) Within two months, I got the money. I was elated, because I thought I could finally leave the country.

But the next day, that girl came to my apartment. She said she was pregnant with my child. She said it was illegal to have an abortion in Malaysia, unless pregnancy affected the woman's health. In addition, impregnating someone's wife was punished by the street law. That meant Aidan could punish me in any way he wished. So, I accepted my fate.

Kate, I'm not exaggerating when I say Aidan could've had me killed. I know this probably sounds dramatic and crazy, but I promise it's the truth. I don't know what his wife told him, but he didn't interfere with the pregnancy, and for a little while, I started to hope things would work out.

The day Henrik was born was the happiest day of my life. I ran around the neighborhood probably a hundred times. He was the most beautiful baby I'd ever seen. They say that mixed race people are often prettier, and he was no exception. (Kate, that's why you are so beautiful, too.)

Shortly after Henrik was born, though, his mother disappeared. I was too scared to ask Aidan about her. All I could think was, what if Aidan did something to her? Or, what if he gets enraged over the whole situation again and has me killed this time? What if he takes Henrik away from me? I was terrified and confused, and I had no idea how I was going to take care of Henrik by myself. But it was Aidan, again, who offered me a lifeline.

You see, Aidan loved Henrik. Maybe he thought he'd be a terrible father, or maybe he just didn't want the responsibility, I *don't know—but he wanted Henrik close to him, as my son. (He never did forgive me for sleeping with his wife.) He said if I keep working for him, he would provide a full-time babysitter for Henrik. He even agreed to let me go back to school and get an engineering degree because he didn't want Henrik's dad to be stupid… his words, not mine. So I stayed. Raising Henrik has been my life. I tried to run a few times, and I threatened to leave a lot more, but it never worked out. Eventually, I gave up. I was miserable, but I had Henrik.*

Then I met you, Kate. Your words moved me and kept me moving forward. When I saw your picture, I immediately fell in love with you. I told you many times before that it is not easy to come across a woman with a good personality and good appearance. When I fell for you, I vowed to unite with you and spend the rest of my life with you. I have always meant it. I have loved you and will always love you, only you. With Henrik going off to college, I think I might have one last chance to get away from Aidan and make it to your side.

But… I stopped chatting with other women as soon as I started talking to you, which means Aidan hasn't made any profits off of me for months. That means I'm right back where I started: owing Aidan money. But I don't want to scam you, or anyone else, ever again.

So, my love, I must ask you this. Please send me $5,000, so that I can pay Aidan and get out of here. When I see you in California, I'll certainly pay you back. Please believe me and trust me on this… or at least tell me if you can't forgive me. I just need to know.

I love you and hope to hold you in my arms soon.
Love,
Edward Jónsson

P.S. You might have wondered why Henrik and I don't have the same last name. In Iceland, parents and children often do not bear the same last name. Before Henrik was born, Aidan demanded that he not share his wife's last name, so... we did it my way.

Kate and Henrik couldn't say a word for a long time. They looked at each other, as if each of them was trying to comprehend what they just finished reading. Quietly, Kate passed the letter around to Dominique and Tren, who shared it with William and Laura. Everyone was stunned by its contents.

Kate hesitated, but soon said, "I'll send him $5,000 tomorrow."

"You will? Really?" Henrik looked surprised.

"Yes, we need to get your father out of there. He's suffered too long, and all by himself..." Kate could feel herself getting choked up. She couldn't believe how much Edward had suffered and sacrificed, all for a simple mistake in his youth. All because he had wanted to be a good father to his son.

"I'll never forget this, Mrs. Smi— Kate. I'll pay you back when I have a job," Henrik promised. Kate could see he was overwhelmed, too. But then, Dominique cut in.

"No, mom, you don't have to worry about it. Remember, I said he emailed me?"

"Yes, but–how did he get your email address?"

Dominique smiled sheepishly. "Well, he seemed to miss his son so much and he looked like he really wanted to come to California, so... I gave it to him. Anyway, more importantly–he emailed me not long ago, and he said not to worry about the money, and just to wait for him a little more. I don't know what happened, but I think... I think he might be on his way."

Kate and Henrik looked at each other, shocked. Was Edward… coming to California?

****

Edward couldn't wait for Dominique to read his email. He couldn't wait for Henrik to find Kate and give her the letter. In fact, he was done waiting for anyone else, ever again. It was time to take matters into his own hands, and Aidan couldn't stop him any longer. He would find a way to pay Aidan himself. But he was going to California. But first, he was going to say goodbye.

He cleaned the house as much as he could. He packed his suitcase and brought it down to leave it by the front door. Edward would be leaving in the evening, but he had one last stop to make--the hospital where Aidan was being treated for his burns. It had begun to rain shortly after Edward got home, but now it was sunny out. Edward walked to the hospital, thinking of what he would say to Kate when they united. The walk to the hospital was a slight uphill, but Edward didn't mind it at all and he didn't mind the humidity, either.

As he reached the hospital entrance, he went straight to the reception and asked for Aidan Nik. The nurse told him that the patient was on the third floor, room 217. Edward thanked her and took the stairs. Another nurse guided him there and knocked on the door gently. "Come in," came from the inside. Edward opened the door and slowly walked into the room. Aidan smiled when he saw Edward.

"Hey, Edward."

"Hey, Aidan. How are you feeling?"

"Oh, this is nothing… Ouch! Hehehe…"

The nurse walked out of the room, leaving Edward and Aidan alone.

Edward took a deep breath. "I came here to tell you that…"

"… that you are leaving," Aidan interrupted, finishing the sentence. He didn't seem surprised.

"Yeah, I'm leaving this evening for good." Strangely enough, Edward didn't feel afraid. For so many years, he had been terrified and paranoid, trying to protect Henrik and himself. But looking at Aidan lying in the hospital bed, he didn't feel any of that. He only felt that he was finally doing what he should've done a long time ago. "I wanted to thank you for all you did for Henrik. I'll never forget it."

"Ah, shut up, you probably hated me all these years. But I always thought you were like my brother. So, where you going?"

"California. Henrik is there."

"Right, I knew he wasn't going to college in Iceland." Aidan sounded amused. Edward felt a little embarrassed for thinking he could pull one over on Aidan, but it didn't matter anymore. "How is he doing?"

"He is doing very well, thanks."

"Well, it's my turn to thank you. You saved my life, and I'll never forget that, either."

"You're welcome."

Edward and Aidan looked at each other for a few seconds but said nothing. Then, Aidan broke the silence. "It's been twenty years, huh? Time flies."

"Yeah, you can say that again."

"We went through ups and downs together…"

"Yeah, we did." Silence fell again; Edward was lost in thought, and it seemed like Aidan was too.

Eventually, Aidan said, "Well, you take care, okay?"

"Yeah, I will. You too, okay?" Edward got up. "Aidan, I'll

wire you the money I owe you when I settle down in California."

"The money?" Aidan looked confused for a minute, but then recognition dawned on his face. "Oh, with your girl? Just forget about it. You saved my life, man."

Edward was momentarily speechless. He stared at Aidan for a few seconds, but he could only quietly manage to say, "Thank you."

Edward headed to the door, but Aidan spoke up one more time. "Oh yeah, I got a postcard from Iceland yesterday. It was from 'Henrik,' but it wasn't his handwriting. Tell your parents not to worry about sending any more postcards. Nice trick, though."

Aidan laughed, and Edward couldn't help it; he laughed too. It was a bizarre feeling, being on good terms with Aidan after so many years, but he was glad to leave the country on a positive note. He hurried home, feeling liberated.

He sent an email to Henrik telling him that he would be arriving in San Francisco the next day. He put his laptop in the suitcase he'd left by the front door. He then glanced around the house one last time. *Twenty years of my life in this house,* Edward thought, feeling a bit of nostalgia. He shook his head and picked up the suitcase, and soon he was on his way to the airport.

****

Edward was coming to California.

Henrik had contacted her earlier to confirm it. They would be going to San Francisco to pick Edward up in the afternoon, which meant Kate only had the morning to prepare. It felt like too much time and way too soon all at once. She tried to go through her normal daily routines, but her mind was stuck on Edward; she didn't even bother trying to work. She could hardly believe that she was finally going to meet Edward in person, just as she'd dreamed of for so many months.

The first impression was very crucial, as they say; thus, she wanted to make it right. "Should I just say 'hi' or 'hi Edward'... Should I speak first or let him speak first?" she mumbled as she bathed. As she went back and forth with the wording, she felt like she was a schoolgirl going on her first date. The bath helped; when she finally came out of the tub, she felt more relaxed. She dried her hair and put on a little makeup, then dressed in her favorite beige dress. She was all set with her favorite earrings and gold bracelet.

Around eleven, the doorbell rang. "Who could that be?" she wondered. She went downstairs and saw no sign of William or Laura; they were probably still sleeping. She opened the door to find Henrik. "Henrik, I thought I would pick you up in about two hours. What happened?"

"Nothing, I just couldn't wait for you at the dorm, so I called a Lyft to get here."

Kate smiled at Henrik, who looked very handsome in a blue button-down shirt and gray sweater. "I totally understand how you're feeling. I was already ready myself, even though we still have a few hours until he arrives." Kate chuckled, and Henrik did too. "Are you hungry?"

"Um... as a matter of fact, yes, because I didn't eat my breakfast... Hehehe..."

"C'mon in. I'll fix us some sandwiches."

Kate went to the kitchen and put an apron on. She made them both some tuna sandwiches, deciding she would brush her teeth one more time before they left; she would have to touch up her makeup anyway, since she'd gotten ready so early.

As they ate, she said, "You must be thrilled to see your father again. How long has it been since you left home?"

"Um, I left home at the end of May, so… seven months?"

"Wow, that's a long time. But the day has finally come." Kate said it out loud, just to hear it for herself again too.

"Yeah, I second that." Henrik smiled at her, and she looked back at him warmly.

"You know what? When I first saw you at Jane's house, I felt something familiar about you, and you reminded me of someone. But I couldn't figure out why. Then I remembered I saw your picture on Facebook, way back when your father first messaged me. I wish I'd realized it then, so we could have freed your father much sooner," Kate said, feeling a little regretful.

"Me too. When Mike introduced you as Kate, my heart kind of jumped, and I felt something warm about you. But when you introduced yourself as Kate Smith, I was disappointed, you know…"

"Yes, I know. I don't know why I picked that exact night to go back to using my maiden name. This is really all my fault, isn't it?" But instead of feeling upset or guilty, Kate could only laugh at the absurdity of it all.

"Right, the important thing is that I found you, and my dad is on his way to unite with us."

"Yes, that is the most important thing. And I'm so glad that it all worked out well in the end."

Kate and Henrik exchanged a happy, content look. Then Kate asked, "What time did you say your father is arriving?"

"1:00 pm."

"Right, then we'd better get going."

"Yeah, let's go!"

The northbound of the 101 freeway in the early afternoon was not congested, and they arrived at the airport in no time. They arrived with approximately thirty minutes to spare, leaving Kate with plenty of time to park. There were many people in the terminal when they arrived: those who were departing; those who were arriving; and those who were sending people off. And then, those who were there to greet someone, like Kate and Henrik. This was the third time that Kate had been to this airport in a year: her trip to Southeast Asia, Dominique and Tren's, and now this. As she was reflecting on the events of the year, Henrik's voice brought her out of her reverie.

"What are you thinking, Kate?"

"Oh, I was just reflecting about what's happened this year. It's been a lot." She smiled at him. "But perhaps, the best thing is that we are greeting your father today."

"Yeah." Henrik smiled at her. "What are you going to say to him when you see him?"

"Um, I don't know… I don't even know if I'm ready to meet him…"

"Oh, I'm sure you are. Just be yourself, he already loves you."

"Just be myself." That wasn't so different from what Edward had told her over the months they'd spoken. "Thanks, Henrik. You have really grown up, even in just the past seven months."

"Thanks, Kate."

Then, it was time to head to baggage claim. As they passed the newsstand, Henrik suddenly started running, leaving Kate behind. Kate walked slowly, feeling very nervous. Soon she saw him wave his both hands high up in the air. She could hear him shout, "Dad! Dad! Over here!" She stopped in place, as if her feet were glued to the floor. In the far distance, she saw Henrik hug Edward, father and son both all smiles and tears. They exchanged a few words and started walking toward Kate. She felt even more nervous and wanted to hide herself somewhere. But she couldn't move. Edward's gaze landed on her, and he didn't look away as they approached.

When they were a few feet away from her, Henrik said proudly, "Kate, this is my dad, Edward Jónsson. Dad, this is Kate Fleming–no, Kate Smith."

Then, Kate heard clapping and cheers some distance away. The three of them looked over; Kate saw all her loved ones. Dominique and Tren, William and Laura, Miki and James, Sara and Eric, Jane and Mike, Mary, and even Liam had come to support her long-awaited meeting, and all of them were smiling and cheering.

Edward had eyes only for her. When Kate looked back at him, he was still gazing at her affectionately. Finally, he spoke, and she heard his voice at last.

"Hi Kate."

She said with an equal affection, "Hi Edward."

They continued to gaze at each other, as Henrik looked on, smiling.

--End--

Printed in the USA
CPSIA information can be obtained
at www.ICGtesting.com
LVHW091117170424
777534LV00002B/290

9 798218 332617